continued . . .

"While her subjects range from nightmare time-shares in Dana Point to the horror of being the Woman's Day speaker at Venice High, Loh is especially attuned to the difference in L.A.'s constantly shifting class structure. . . . Nowhere is Loh better than in deflating the pretensions of the L.A. cultural scene. It's about time that someone took on the periphery of Los Angeles with such wicked delight, because—face it—in this town, the periphery's the real heart of the city."

—*Los Angeles Times*

"A hilarious lampoon of Hollywood, the Valley and the whole L.A. scene: the industry, the people, the self-absorption."

—*USA Today*

"The definitive collection of her work."

—*Buzz*

Praise for
Aliens in America

"Absorbing . . . hilarious . . . a world in which everyone feels, at times, like an alien in America."

—*Los Angeles Times*

"Loh's ill-matched parents—a cheap, passive-aggressive, serial-marrying Chinese father and a towering, peach-schnapps-drinking, party-loving German mother—were brought together by the vagaries of history and a shiny Buick; Loh, a typical Southern Californian daughter, wonders where she figures in the equation. The three engaging vignettes in her autobiographical monologue are driven by intelligence and the healing power of expressive fury."

—*The New Yorker*

"At once deeply personal and broadly universal . . . In three stories—told from the perspectives of childhood, late adolescence and young adulthood—she describes the awkwardness of trying to fit together her parents' diverse cultures (Dad is Chinese, Mom is German), while figuring out where she herself fits in the great American scheme of things."

—*Los Angeles Daily News*

"Ms. Loh's story is both exceptional and very familiar. As her performance piece develops, in three self-contained sections, it becomes clear that her tale is less one of cultural conflict than of universal isolation."

—*The New York Times*

"Terrifically wry, literate, self-revealing, and pointed."

—*The Village Voice*

if you

lived here,

you'd be home

by now

_____

sandra

tsing

loh

riverhead books ▪ new york

RIVERHEAD BOOKS
Published by The Berkley Publishing Group
A member of Penguin Putnam Inc.
200 Madison Avenue
New York, New York 10016

First Riverhead hardcover edition: September 1997
First Riverhead trade paperback edition: September 1998
Riverhead trade paperback ISBN: 1-57322-695-5

The Penguin Putnam Inc. World Wide Web site address is
http://www.penguinputnam.com

The Library of Congress has catalogued the Riverhead hardcover edition
as follows:

Loh, Sandra Tsing.
If you lived here, you'd be home by now : a novel / Sandra Tsing Loh.
p.   cm.
ISBN 1-57322-068-X
I. Title.
PS3562.0459I48   1997   97-10056 CIP
813'.54—dc21

Printed in the United States of America

10   9   8   7   6   5   4   3   2   1

For Mike Miller,
my favorite South Dakotan
tax disadvantage

part one

———

gridlands

tujunga

When NPR clicked on that morning at eight—"From Washington, I'm Korva Coleman"—Bronwyn Peters broke into a scream.

My God, she thought, hurtling upward toward consciousness. Why am I screaming? She blinked open her eyes.

And found that once again, she was cringing against a rock-hard futon, coddled by warmish, slightly musty-smelling sheets. To her left was a battered Kaypro computer, hunched on the chipped child's desk Paul had bought at a garage sale. To her right, grimy yellow light fell through a glass slat window fringed by a ragged beige curtain half falling off its hooks. Above, a brown swing-arm lamp that was held together with duct tape collapsed in on itself, like a buzzard.

This was Bronwyn's living situation in Los Angeles—the nightmare from which, it seemed, she would never wake. She closed her eyes to suppress another scream.

"But don't you find cheesy Southern California tract houses like this hilarious?" Paul had asked six years ago, while convincing her that they should rent this falling-down three-bedroom in

Tujunga. Tujunga was not even on the outskirts of Los Angeles, it was the petticoat of some distant . . . mountain range. Which was . . . the San Fernandos? The San Bernardinos? All Bronwyn knew was that this Tujunga was forty minutes—five freeways—away from the city . . .

Which was the whole point. Paul had pushed up his black Elvis Costello glasses, fingers splayed with intensity. "Don't you see? Being out here is so Lancaster Desert, so Frank Zappa-esque! It's like living *in* Los Angeles but refusing to be a part of it. Like starting our own tribe. Denying that whole fou-fou trendy La Brea/Melrose/giving-over-to-the-style-weasels thing. And besides"—here he became boyish, endearingly hopeful—"look at all this space! We could never have afforded this in San Francisco.

"Here . . ." He'd pressed forward. "This can become like some kind of a screening room, or home theater–type place." He snapped the light on in the mildewy converted garage which, though it cradled two rusted bikes and three bags of laundry at the time, seemed fixable.

His voice trilled upward, sunny: "And this can be a darkroom. For your photography! Which I know you will go back to, eventually . . ." He swung open the door to an odd little thing that was somewhere between a quarter- and a half-bathroom.

Bronwyn had coined it a three-eighths bathroom and they had laughed and kissed, buoyed by Paul's enthusiasm, and the raffish confidence of youth.

"And here is where *I* will work." His tone became grave as they stepped down into the screened-in lanai.

His work. This they did not joke about. Not anymore.

Because since entering his M.F.A. program, the change in Paul's writing had been nothing short of phenomenal. Gone were the imitative, juvenile sketches. This new work was poignant, strong, mature. This sudden blossoming of Paul's Talent had been something totally unexpected, the breaking of a new dawn over the jumbled landscape of their twenties, which had been a rooty, twisted terrain pocked by odd little dead ends: "Maybe I'll go back to school in fashion photography" (Bronwyn), "Maybe I should start a punk band" (Paul), "Maybe we should move to Boulder, Colorado, and start a farm" (both).

"I just feel as though something inside me . . . has broken loose," he'd said seriously to her, taking her hands, one evening.

The new Paul was a fury of production, writing short stories, plays, even a film script, winning award after award from his M.F.A. program as though knocking down bowling pins. And then it came. Just before graduation, behind the closed doors of Professor Donald Carroll, Paul was bequeathed the name of an actual agent. Paul and only Paul had received this boon, none of the others—not Susan Mitiyama, not Henry Marcus, not even Jasper T. Jones with his quirky brilliant Hunter S. Thompson–type stuff. Only Paul was so anointed.

And so, from that day on, a deeper, unspoken pact had begun to form between them. That Paul's Talent was a sacred thing, a primal thing, a thing larger than their love. But it could root their love. Yes. That was it. Paul's Talent could be the vast underground continent that anchored the floating buoys of their life. One night when Bronwyn, helpless with giggles, had slid to the floor off of torn ratty pillows, the thought had flown out of him: "The first thing we're going to do when I sell something is buy a new couch!"

It was a joke, but both saw that underneath this joking was a promise. What Paul was saying was, these in fact would be the milestones of their life:

First story. Second book. Third script.

The marriage. The family. The future.

And so, on that first day in Tujunga, and her first day in Los Angeles, Bronwyn had taken the hand of her love, her brilliant love, as they stood in the stairwell, quiet, in awe of the possibilities.

"Look at all this space," Paul had repeated, gesturing at the house.

Yes, there was a lot of space, Bronwyn was thinking now, six years later almost to the day. She pulled herself resignedly to a sitting position, back against the wall. In the old days, feeling like this in the morning, she would have lit up a cigarette, but of course she'd quit all that a long time ago. From the overturned milk crate they used as a nightstand, NPR continued to murmur from the Panasonic clock radio: "In Washington today, the House Ways and Means Committee met with President Bush to discuss plans to implement a new tax incentive that . . ." Bronwyn closed her eyes, feeling the suffocating warmth of the sun like a mitt on her face.

Space this house had, sure. Endless corridors of faux hardwood paneling faintly greenish under the fluorescents. Wide gently rippling deltas of Aztec sunburst linoleum. Huge swatches of shag rug in blood orange, harvest gold, avocado green . . .

Older and wiser, Bronwyn now saw 23511 Colton Place for what it was. A horror. A grotesquerie. Unsalvageable.

"And with such a huge yard, maybe you can start that herb garden you're always talking about!" Paul had said.

Herb garden? All there was here was a bald, rocky lawn stubbled with yellow weeds and chain-link fence . . .

Frank Zappa-esque? No, 23511 Colton Place was more David Lynch than Frank Zappa. It was the sort of place where a querulous old woman with an eye patch would live with her inbred adult son, Hank, clad in a big old diaper. It was the kind of place you saw featured on *A Current Affair,* where an axe murder had been committed by—

At that precise moment, as if to push the point home, the pumping disco beat of one of Jonathan's favorite groups, Frankie Goes to Hollywood, began to rock the house.

Bronwyn squeezed her eyes tightly shut.

Jonathan.

Jonathan, of course, was more her fault than Paul's. Paul's older brother, Jonathan, had originally come to visit L.A. for a week.

"Just a week?" Bronwyn had said to Jonathan, that fateful evening, as they companionably drank jug Gallo wine in silhouette against the orange, mauve, chartreuse, toasted hazelnut L.A. sunset. Jonathan had been pouring out his litany of troubles to her: how the hard-won Ph.D. in French horn performance at prestigious Oberlin College meant nothing, what with there being so few seats in today's symphonies, the endless hassles with all the political bullshit, the auditions, the kowtowing, the travel.

Bronwyn found, in the midst of this monologue, that she did not really like Jonathan—his shock of oddly matted dark hair, the small eyes glittering behind the glasses, the lack of chin, his odd habit of sniffing the tips of his long nervous fingers. And yet, she had so much love for Paul, her brilliant Paul, that it seemed right that her love should overflow onto all of the Hoffsteads—Hub, Dorothy, Jonathan—even though none seemed remotely like him.

And so, through the rosy lens of love, Bronwyn saw Jonathan —brother, after all, to the Anointed—as a brilliant person just temporarily down on his luck.

"You're staying just a week?" she had repeated to Jonathan.

"You said *what?*" Paul hissed later.

Of course, within days of their companionable Gallo char-treuse sunset conversation, Bronwyn realized her tragic mistake. In truth, Jonathan was like a virus. Given the proverbial inch, Jonathan now grafted himself and his chronic unemployment onto their defenseless host household like an unwanted third head. And now here he was underfoot, the moldy fungus of him, smoking pot in his bathrobe and reading old *L.A. Times*es, which he now busily, like an autistic savant on some dark obsessive project, began to stack in the converted garage, aka what was supposed to be becoming the home theater.

"I just think you would be more comfortable in your own place," was how Bronwyn had put it, after the first month.

"But look at all this extra space you have," Jonathan had argued, brandishing his Jabba the Hut coffee mug.

That was two years ago.

And of course it was true.

The space. Bronwyn and Paul had all of that space.

PUMPA PUMPA PUMPA! went the Frankie Goes to Holly-wood record. PUMPA PUMPA PUMPA!

Bronwyn took a deep teary breath—and did the only thing she could do, for the moment.

"Shut up!" she screamed. "Shut up!"

The door flew open.

Paul, in his customary T-shirt and karate pants, shot to her side.

"Bronwyn! Are you okay?"

Bronwyn's phrases jerked out of her in short anguished blats.

"It's just . . . the way we live here . . . it's—it's horrible! With Jonathan . . . the futons . . . the stacks of *L.A. Times*es . . . this filthy house . . ."

"I know, Noni, I know," he murmured, eyes cloudy behind his glasses, rubbing his hand worriedly against the small of her back.

"Why do we still . . . live in L.A.? Why can't we just move?"

Paul's posture did not change, but his hand stopped rubbing. "We can't leave," he said, quiet. "Your Ph.D. program is here."

She turned to him, wild-eyed. "It doesn't have to be. I have an application in for that—that Connecticut thing. You know I do. Westbury College. We can be out of here in six months—"

That was it: her plan of escape. Westbury, Connecticut.

Westbury College was the very opposite of Los Angeles. You could see that from the brochure. It was white clapboard cottages. It was rolling green hills. It was a cluster of blackberries trembling leafy in the sun, the reassuring scrape-scrape-scrape of a wooden cart, the faint distant clang of a bell, a susurrus of wind. It could be, upon completion of Bronwyn's Ph.D. in Women's Studies, $38,000 a year.

"It could be good for you too, sweetie. Maybe you could get a teaching job at Westbury College as well—The Nineteenth-Century Novel, something you'd really enjoy . . ." She pressed on hurriedly: "Which would still give you plenty of time to write!"

The hand dropped away from her back.

"They even have a theater there!" Her vocal pitch sailed high with hope. "With the support of the university, I'll bet you could put up some of your plays. It'll be much easier than in Los Angeles!"

Three years ago, one of Paul's plays had been accepted for a showcase at Theater 405, a tiny equity-waiver theater so named because of its proximity to the 405 Freeway. Wild with excitement, Bronwyn and Paul spent almost $300 on fliers, sent them all out with handwritten notes. Because of the $18 ticket price, though, only nine people showed at the opening, four of them from Bronwyn's Women's Studies department. However, by incredible coincidence, one of them was an enthusiastic *L.A. Times* stringer named Leonard Dabro. But the two-paragraph review Mr. Dabro eventually wrote ran not in the *L.A. Times* but in something called *Westside Eye*. Nonetheless, the Theater 405 owner, a man by the name of John Gallin, was excited enough by the write-up to say he would put up Paul's play again in the fall.

One month later, John Gallin had a nervous breakdown.

And so it went, the cavalcade of disappointments, the loop-the-loops of the roller-coaster ride becoming ever more small, squalid, sad. One day, Bronwyn returned to their VW bus after helping John Gallin move his furniture into a tinier, more claustrophobic apartment in Culver City (he had long since lost his lease on the theater), only to see a $38 parking ticket waiting for her on the windshield. It was at this particular point that she thought, No more. No more.

She had reached the end of her rope with L.A. and the struggling people they had to deal with in it—the crust of disappointment they had all over them, the wild-eyed, sunburned despair.

Dignity. That's all she wanted from their lives. Dignity.

"I think Westbury might be a better place for you to work on your novel," she said softly. "You know, much more quiet. Think about it. A beautiful old library. Literary peers. Walks in the woods."

Paul turned away from the window.

"It's just ... everything in L.A. moves so fast. Everyone is judged in a split second. A split second. And it's over."

What she really wanted to say was: At age thirty in Los Angeles, we're failures. At age forty in Westbury, Connecticut, though, we'd be just starting to become interesting. That's the point. We need to move to a place where success is judged according to a more . . . geologic time scale.

"I'm not doing the novel anymore," he said abruptly.

Her body recoiled as if hit.

"What? But . . . I see you at that computer all day, always working . . ."

"You can't sell a first novel," he said. "And even when you do . . . You know that Brad Lin only got three thousand dollars for his?"

"Three thousand?" The figure struck a terrible chord within her. That book had taken Brad three years. "Are you sure?"

"I won't ever be able to make us money at that."

"And so what are you . . ."

"I'm writing a spec script."

She did not dare to utter a sound, not even trusting herself to swallow.

Oh no, she thought. Oh no.

She finally found her tongue.

"But I thought you weren't going to try that Hollywood stuff anymore. It makes you feel so dark, so miserable, so terrible . . . It's about everything you're not, sweetie."

"I know you don't think I can do this." He sat back down on the futon, took her hands. "But I can. I'm going to be much more practical this time. I'm not going to get all pissed off again. That phase is way, way behind me. I've grown up now. I've grown up."

"I just . . . Your temperament isn't really suited for—"

"The trick is," he said now, pushing up his black glasses, "to set my sights low. Really low. I've become really practical now, Noni.

1 1

I'm a changed person. I know that the answer is not the high people in Hollywood. It's the low people."

Bronwyn said nothing.

"The problem is, everything I've aimed for in the past has been too glitzy. My futuristic rewrite of *Citizen Kane* idea, for instance . . . I mean, that's ridiculous. No one is going to pay me to do that. Ever. In fact"—Here he narrowed his eyes, his voice becoming dreamy—"I've come to think there's this kind of . . . Gatekeeper of Success who punishes artists for their hubris. You know. So even if I did get some kind of meeting at Paramount about the *Citizen Kane* thing—that's the moment you should hunker down in crash position, waiting for the cataclysmic fall."

He stood up again, began to pace, his fingers tracing the air for emphasis in circles and points.

"But an industrial? A Motorola safety spot, a high school health video, an infomercial for the AARP? That's just unglamorous enough to—to maybe not fall through. An industrial is not so outrageously glitzy that the Gatekeeper of Success will deny us. 'All right,' he'll say gruffly, searching our bags. 'Not much here. All you've got is a basket of lentils and laundry. And you're only going as far as Barstow.' " Paul yanked his thumb. " 'Let 'em through.' "

"Is this . . . really what you want to do?" Bronwyn asked, bewildered, and for the first time, truly worried.

"I'm just trying to wipe the cobwebs from my eyes." He turned back to her. "I mean, look. Pittsburgh has steel. Detroit has cars. Los Angeles has film and stuff. You can almost see the same smokestacks, making everything sooty. It's an industry. It's not necessarily glamorous. Like all the other workers in the U.S., I just have to heave my pick over my shoulder and go to work.

"And even though I hate it, I know we have to start going out more. Meeting contacts. Hooking up with them."

He held up a party invite. It flashed pink and neon and everything scary.

"Oh Paul," she murmured, her arms stealing around him as though to shield him from a coming hurricane. "Oh Paul."

where's

the party?

"I'm glad you decided to go with the black jacket. It looks nice—very, very nice," Bronwyn whispered to Paul, giving him a quick supportive nod as they bobbed ever so slightly forward in the line of black-clad partygoers.

In truth, as soon as Bronwyn had glimpsed the spectacle unfolding before them, she'd felt the usual wave of uncertainty and dread. Tonight's party, sponsored by a trendy downtown magazine, was being held at a big, echoing place called Spa Downtown. But in a classic Los Angeles marketing twist, this was not a dance club but a brand-new, ultraexpensive health club.

Looking up, one saw that all around the central pink-pulsing mambo area rose these gleaming, quasi-Dantesque rings of fitness. One floor up, behind glass walls, a ghostly row of investment bankers strained at their Lifecycles, grim as a military phalanx. Above that was the next *bolgia,* brightly lit, its tiny bald denizens struggling under black handle-grip bars, metal cables, shining dumbbells. Above that was the track.

Looking down, one saw the packed, writhing dance floor,

columns of pink light playing over bobbing heads that were screaming: *"Mambo! Mambo!"* Trays of Flaming Kiwi Sunsets and mango chipotle shrimp twirled by. All around, festooning the walls and eaves, papier-mâché parrots dusted with snow and Cuban devil masks draped with plastic holly necklaces dangled, turquoise neon lights sparkling up the tinsel.

Christmas in Los Angeles—always a decorative season.

Given such circumstances, Bronwyn actually had no clue as to whether Paul's jacket was okay. He was wearing his regulation black, the black that had served him so well, lo these many years. But Bronwyn couldn't shake the impression that his cool black jacket with narrow leather lapels had these . . . two faint, crescent-shaped sags around the shoulders. As though passing hors d'oeuvre trays had been lunged at one too many times.

She craned her neck to look at the other guests.

But all she saw about her was this dark, endlessly black ocean of Los Angeles' vast undocumented hip. It brought on, like a wave, the feeling she so often had at clubs—that living in Los Angeles was like being an extra in a movie that was starring other people entirely.

"It's a nice jacket," she whispered again to Paul.

He squeezed her hand back.

With a resigned heave, Bronwyn and Paul threw their bodies into a kind of Third World–ish human wedge of black-clad people leaning against the backs of people leaning against the backs of the people actually leaning into the bar, who were futilely shouting drink orders at three or four frantic, white-shirted bartenders.

Bronwyn waved her arm at the blond bartender with the slightly punk haircut, who looked as though he could not be much older than nineteen.

"We'd like two Chardonnays!" she cried out.

It seemed that he didn't hear her. His arms pumping like pistons, the blond bartender was methodically shelling ice cubes into glasses, ice cubes into glasses, ice cubes into glasses.

But who were these glasses for? The other bartenders were shelling ice cubes into their own glasses, one at a time, like you'd expect, as they speedily blended and poured and shook and swizzled drinks. Not this guy.

"Excuse me!" Bronwyn yelled. "Excuse me! Sir!"

Still he continued, arms pumping. Ice cubes into glasses, ice cubes into glasses, ice cubes into glasses.

"Hey!" Bronwyn's arm shot out like a pinion and grabbed his bicep. "You! Excuse me! We'd like two Chardonnays!"

The bartender put the glass down with deliberate slowness, mouth slack, and indicated a white, computer-printed card taped to the end of the bar.

" 'Sod People Performance,' " Bronwyn read. "I don't get it."

The bartender sighed, looked off to one side as though seeking escape from this tawdry, impossible world, and decided to break what was apparently a vow of silence.

"Sod People," he intoned. "I'm part of the Sod People." He waved at the illuminated bottles behind him, the mob of guests, the confetti, the wheeling pink spotlights. "This is a performance. I'm not really a bartender. I'm just performing the motions. The Sod People . . ." He leaned forward to make his point. "We're *ambient*."

Bronwyn shrugged to signal her nonplus, stretched forward to slip a copy of *LA LA* magazine (the evening's host organization) off the edge of the polished wood counter.

She held it before her, studied the cover, dejected. It was a photo of Madonna's breasts in their pointy Sno-Kone bra.

"What's this supposed to be?" she wondered aloud.

"It's a statement about celebrity covers!" somebody shouted at them. "Other magazines might carry a cover photo of Isabella Rossellini or Julia Roberts! *LA LA* magazine's point is that by now, Madonna's breasts have themselves become a celebrity! What they're wearing, how they're shot—the breasts *themselves* have become a cultural indicator!"

"Henry!" Paul cried out. Bronwyn and Paul turned to the speaker, or really, the yeller—Paul's fellow struggling Writer's Program alum.

As usual, Henry wore the tweed cap, ironically distant "Impeach Nixon" button, wispy goatee. As usual, Henry looked tickled to be alive, a cork bobbing perennially, impossibly, atop untroubled waters.

"What is it with this 'List'?" Bronwyn asked Henry—more crabbily than she felt, because she was really very relieved to see a familiar face. She flopped her *LA LA* magazine at him like a wet towel. "It looks like it's supposed to be a list of, like, cool people, but it just doesn't make sense."

"Isn't it maddening?" Henry agreed. "It's complete chaos! Which is, in a way, when you think about it, really brilliant."

"George Clinton, Anjelica Huston, John Waters," Bronwyn read. "All certifiably cool people."

"Yeah, but look down here . . ." Paul joined into the game. "Farrah Fawcett? Debbie Gibson? And here . . . John Malkovich, *on* the list—but crossed out!"

"And here's Jamie Lee Curtis," Bronwyn added, "crossed out!"

"But how the hell did she get *on* in the first place?" Paul protested. "Was there a sudden Jamie Lee Curtis publicity blip—after *Perfect* and before *Blue Steel*—that we missed?"

"I personally believe this list is made out by some seventeen-year-old unpaid intern in New York," Henry offered. "Maybe even a monkey!"

"Hey!" Paul cried out, as a large figure shoved into him.

It was a six-foot, four-inch elf sporting bright red lipstick, five-o'clock shadow, fur-trimmed red mini, torn black fishnets, and spike heels. He appeared to be bald under his pointed elf cap, which had the words "LA LA" stenciled across the front, to sad effect. He dragged a red sack of who knew what sorts of dismal Christmas treats behind him. His pudgy face carried an expression of absolute fury.

"Hey, yourself!" the elf snapped, and shoved on.

"An unshaven, two-hundred-pound queen," Henry said. "How very Highways."

"Personally, he makes me think of Santa . . . Santa Monica and Western, that is," Paul parried.

"Hip people," Henry sang, beginning to mambo in place. "*A* list, who's hot."

"Not me!" Paul erupted.

"Not hardly!" Henry guffawed.

"Ha ha ha ha!"

The two would-be writers fell heavily against each other, laughing.

"I miss you, man," Paul said, clapping Henry on the back. "I miss everything."

"Yeah," Henry replied. "I know what you mean."

———

Bronwyn took her place behind the long, snaking line of women that led into the rest room. The Spa Downtown buzz had grown to a roar: wave after wave of sound was hitting her. *"Mambo!"* the crowd screamed. *"Mambo!"*

God, it was good to see Paul have fun. And especially with Henry. Tch. How lighthearted and hilarious Paul used to be before . . . well, before he started to yell. She sighed.

The yelling began . . . when? Just after graduation, probably. When Paul had first called the office of the agent. She remembered the sheer ballsy confidence of him at the time—his invoking Professor Donald Carroll, the writing program, the fact he had won the Robert P. Sloan Screenwriting Award. "Sure! Send us a sample!" piped the assistant. Bronwyn and Paul had danced off to Kinko's and lovingly xeroxed—he handing, she stacking—page after page of his screenplay like elves spinning gold. Not wanting to wait for the mail, they'd hopped into the VW bus and rushed the manuscript right to Beverly Hills so the agent would have it by lunch.

Five months later, it came back with a card:

> *Sorry—*
> *Couldn't get past the first 10 pages—*
> *Too much dialogue*
> *Too much description*
> *My best to Donald Carroll—*
>
> > *K.S.*

"The good thing is that the guy at least remembers Donald Carroll," Bronwyn had posited, not wanting Paul to feel too let down, "so there's still that connection." When Paul didn't say anything, she'd plugged the gaping hole of his silence with more ideas. "And show me anything in that note that says he won't consider *another* script." Still nothing. "Obviously," she'd concluded finally, stoutly, "the door is still open!"

Later, at a party in Echo Park, a slightly drunk Bronwyn had made the mistake of waving a wineglass and using the phrase "Paul's agent." It was at that moment, right in front of all their friends, that Paul exploded.

"God, Bronwyn! Don't you know the note means nothing? It means nothing! These assholes don't ever *read* anything! It's because they're all totally fucking illiterate!"

"Actually, some of the production people I've talked to at Hanelle Sherwood Films have been pretty friendly," Henry had offered. "Maybe you can—"

"No offense, but why would I want to? Why would I want to write fucking business-training videos?" Paul swept on, incinerating even the faintest offer of professional help. Henry's mouth hung open in amazement. Even his "Impeach Nixon" button seemed to droop.

"But it was a really nice note!" Bronwyn protested in horror, trying to turn a hose on the fireball Paul had suddenly become. "It was really—"

"Don't you understand, Bronwyn? The note means nothing! It's a rejection, right? Who are you trying to impress? Why do you always have to exaggerate everything?"

The shock of it, the humiliation. She had burst into tears, run from the house.

Of course he had chased after her. Of course he had caught her, right there on Alvarado. Of course he had flung his arms around her, stroked her hair back as the honking filthy cars blew by, whispering, "I'm sorry, Noni. I'm sorry. I'm sorry."

So the scars healed and yet . . . not quite. That was when Bronwyn began to fear this Hollywood thing . . . because it made Paul's behavior so erratic. It was like this little devil that rode him. Each encounter with the Other, as he often called it—the referral, the returned phone call, the scribbled note—made Paul giddy at first. But in a kind of odd, gurgling, cock-of-the-walk kind of way, not necessarily her beloved's most attractive face.

And then of course, this giddiness would always give away to disappointment. But never a soulful, bluesy, philosophical disappointment.

The Hollywood disappointment was the opposite of cathartic. It was more of a dark, roiling thing that gnawed at a person for months, causing them to pace around the house and deliver a lot of bitten-off "Tch! Fhh! Kkh!" It was more of a "I didn't even *want* that stupid job and they rejected me for a guy with big hair! Oh what a worm I am! I would sell my mother for a job—but unfortunately my mother doesn't go for very much. Perhaps I should fire the woman playing my mother." Etc.

And paradoxically, the more practice Paul had trying to play this Hollywood game, the worse he got at it. The cavalcade of rejection had gotten so long, so complex, so colorful, so massive—a veritable Macy's Thanksgiving Day Parade of rejection—he could not shake its memory or influence upon him. Paul carried his bitterness with him to even the vaguest little North Hollywood mini-mall lunch meetings.

Through it all, Hollywood remained cruelly emotionless, inert. It was much like the scene in front of her now: a pit that hopeful young people flung themselves into, black-clad body after body after body.

"Cute earrings. What are these? Guatemalan?"

The husky, melodious voice was about five inches behind her. Bronwyn felt a gentle pulling at her left earlobe.

She had an impression of something eggshell-hued, sheathlike, and fluttering behind her, a beacon in a world of lint-covered black. She turned to face narrow chiseled moisturized features framed by Ben Franklin glasses on a chain. These were capped off by a perfect auburn pageboy—but no ordinary pageboy.

In spite of herself, Bronwyn felt a breeze lift inside her when she beheld it.

Because this haircut was a beautiful thing, but subtly, subtly so. The hair was ever so lightly feathered at the temples and neck. There were faint burnt sienna and honey highlights in the crown, a certain subtle lift and movement to the back. The more one studied it, entered it, the more offhandedly perfect this simple pageboy became.

But the Ben Franklin glasses were not concerned with anything like $200 haircuts. Presently their gaze was focused on Bronwyn's left earring, which one perfectly manicured hand fondled and turned with easy, surgical precision even as the crowd continued to jostle forward.

"I don't think I've ever seen these. Fred Segal?"

"Actually, I have no idea *what* country these are from. Maybe Pakistan? I got these at the . . . Four Winds Emporium."

The Four Winds. Bronwyn wished she were there now. At the Four Winds, women in Danskin leotards and karate pants dreamily rolled blue carts down tall, bright aisles bursting with colorful ethniciana. Classical music played. There were Italian votive candles, Indonesian batiks, Guatemalan incense sticks in baskets. Compared to all of this, it was safety. It was order. It was peace.

"I love the Four Winds—it's the only place I feel at home in L.A.," was what came out of Bronwyn now, a bit wanly.

"Four Winds?" The Ben Franklin glasses looked puzzled.

"That big warehouse place off of Barham? With the wicker baskets and wind chimes and—"

What happened next came as a surprise.

All at once the blue eyes behind the Ben Franklin glasses closed, the narrow shoulders swathed in eggshell silk tilted back, and a deep, surprisingly earthy chuckle emerged from perfect Revlon lips. A few of the less expensive haircuts around them turned slightly in, temporarily distracted from their mutual progress to the women's rest room.

Because it was a wonderful chuckle, filled with wine and pasta and grapes and sex, the type that crowns its owner queen of everything earthy, the type of chuckle that's bestowed upon one like a sign of favor, a gift.

"The Four Winds Emporium . . ." the woman marveled to the ceiling, when the chuckle was complete. "They really have everything there now, don't they? And at bargain prices. I *am* amazed.

"That's wonderful," she added quickly to a startled Bronwyn, as though to reassure her that she'd done nothing wrong. "Harold," she called to a tall man standing a few feet beyond them. The man wore black tortoiseshells and flowing gray mane, his statuesque frame clad in black double-breasted Armani. He was leaning against a pillar, listening to an excited gesturing man with a ponytail. He had a pleasantly distant expression.

Without blinking, he tilted his head in his wife's direction. "Yes, lamb."

2 3

The beautiful hand indicated Bronwyn's earrings.

"Don't these remind you of that line I designed for Fred Segal? Not that he ended up taking them, I might add." The woman mugged hilariously for Bronwyn's benefit. "Not that the line wasn't *gorgeous*."

"Fred Segal? What does *he* know? Who shops *there*?" Bronwyn replied, somewhat rhetorically.

"Who indeed? It's all tennis stuff! Terry-cloth headbands! Terrible!"

The woman fixed her oddly light eyes on her.

There was a beat.

"Are—are you a designer?" Bronwyn asked.

"Yes!" the woman declared with a large indulgent smile, suddenly blossoming like a flower. "Petra King. Petra King Designs." She pressed a card into Bronwyn's hand. She became maternal. "Call me if you ever want to see some really *good* stuff. I've got a new line I'm doing with beads. Very provocative." She indicated the man behind her with light fingertips. "That's my husband Harold. Harold *King*," she repeated with the faintest emphasis.

"Hello," Harold King called out, ducking his tousled gray mane slightly. He turned back to his conversation.

"Hi," Bronwyn said, giving a quick dimple.

There was another beat.

Bronwyn sensed that she should probably say more, but the truth was that this name made absolutely no impression on her.

This did not seem to faze Petra King.

It actually seemed to encourage her.

Petra leaned in, confidingly, and began to speak rapidly in what seemed a kind of code.

"It's very unusual, of course, for Harold to let me drag him out on a night like this. It's so close to the AFTRA AARE Awards . . . And you know how it is these days with all of the Paula Abdul hopefuls . . . Even though it's all about MCA/Sony *sound track* . . . All you really want is a nerd who speaks ASCAP, you know? For the others you can go to Alto Palato, end of story . . ."

To Bronwyn, this kind of industry talk always sounded like "Bla bla bla bla bla." For the life of her, she could not follow it. As much as she tried, her attention always flew away like a puppet on a string.

But suddenly—perhaps it was Harold King's beautiful sculpted suit, perhaps it was the four glasses of wine she'd had, perhaps it was Petra's cool hand on hers, gently beckoning, encouraging, even permitting—she heard herself saying: "I'd love you to meet my boyfriend, Paul Hoffstead. He is a very, very wonderful writer. Screenplays." She looked around wildly, but of course Paul and Henry had disappeared from their post.

"Paul who?" Petra queried, frowning a little.

"Paul Hoffstead," Bronwyn answered more loudly, for Harold's benefit as well. "A screenwriter. Very talented."

Petra did not seem surprised, nor was she very warm. "Have we seen anything of his on the screen recently?" she asked.

Harold King and his tousled-mane Harold King–ness seemed to be growing more and more pleasantly distant as the conversation progressed. By now it was as though Bronwyn were seeing him through a fish-eye lens, as though he were standing, his face a blank, some hundred feet from the group. She realized she couldn't sustain her current line of argument, she just couldn't.

Abruptly, she felt Paul's failure coiling around her, enveloping her like a gassy cloud.

"Nope," Bronwyn whispered, feeling the alcohol sour on her breath. "No."

"I'm sure we shall see something of his soon," Petra replied suddenly, with perfect grace, correcting Bronwyn and her self-imposed sense of gassy failure. The mambo music had become deafening. They were almost inside the rest room—its rows of stalls brightly lit, disordered, packed with women and their piles of teased hair. Petra smiled and raised her voice, indicating both easy forgiveness and the end of the discussion.

"Call me if you ever—! New line—! Beads—!"

"What did you say?" Bronwyn screamed. *"What?"*

But the line of women was loosening, pieces of it detaching and spinning off in the rush to find the next empty stall. Petra King waved a last fleeting hand as she wafted away. And this was the way Bronwyn would recall her later, Petra King, cool, iridescent, floating slightly above the world on a cloud of eggshell silk and Bijan.

Bronwyn pushed her way back into the party, wondering if it would be humanly possible for her to find Paul again in this godforsaken building.

She looked up.

And there they were, still working out at almost ten o'clock, the weird avenging angels behind their glass, heads doggedly down, shoulders wrenching forward, their pale banker limbs pumping away forever on their Lifecycles. It brought to Bronwyn's mind those beetle-browed Italian statues who hold up buildings.

Exactly where were they Lifecycling to? she wondered. And why were these people here? No doubt she, Bronwyn, would never really grasp it. Another cool thing she didn't know about. Los Angeles was a universe of rules, ones she would never understand.

"Allee!" the crowd called out, as cameras flashed. "Allee!"

Bronwyn stood on her tiptoes to look over an ocean of dark heads.

"It's time for the celebrities, the celebrities!" she heard herself squeaking, like a sad little cartoon mouse.

And indeed, in a bright spotlight at the door, a woman sporting clown pants and avant-pop hairstyle resembling a hank of fur hanging on one side of her head was waving. Bronwyn recognized Allee Willis from *LA LA* magazine. Apparently Allee Willis owned an enormous collection of fifties Porky the Pig cookie jars. Why this was memorable, Bronwyn did not know.

Behind Allee Willis, ducking the flash, crouched a tiny knot of lesser cast members from *Twin Peaks*—some guy who played one of the policemen, a gas station attendant, a waitress. Why these were the celebrities of the moment, Bronwyn did not know either. She did not even know these people's names. But of course, they must be on some secret list somewhere. If she could only see that list, she would know why.

Over the buzz of the crowd came another sound—a rumble, a roar, a metallic crash. In silhouette, outside the glass panes that had the words "Spa Downtown" sketched in neon across them, bouncers, huge in their Armani jackets, appeared to collide together, then frantically separate. There was the flash of a hundred tiny bulbs going off and a general shout went up:

"Malcolm Forbes!"

At the entrance, in the white glare of the spot, the white-haired patriarch, in black leather jacket and kilt, kickstanded his Harley and eased himself off. He stood and raised his arms up to the throng, as though summoning some kind of dark spirit.

"Where's the party?" he cried out, in guttural tones. "Where's the party?"

All at once, a monsoon of confetti, streamers, and silver balloons fell from the sky. It was an inevitability, a releasing. And finally, after three hours of champing at the bit, a horde of *LA LA* magazine interns in astro-yellow T-shirts were liberated, gushing, onto the floor. They flowed over the mob, handing out the most eagerly awaited tokens of the evening—the promo gift bags.

A bag was pushed onto Bronwyn. Shoulder to shoulder with hundreds of black-clad twenty-something revelers, Bronwyn looked into it, feeling glazed.

And what strange—even poignant—artifacts were inside. A George Michael Christmas cassette, a not-for-individual-sale vial of New West perfume, a slightly bent plastic visor that said "BMW" on it, a Spa Downtown sweatband, a foldout brochure on the Symphony Towers condominium complex, and one, single, lone airline-size bottle of Cointreau.

I guess this is it, she thought morosely. My entire CARE package for the 1990s.

colonial american
women in transition

"Malcolm Forbes on a motorcycle? You're kidding. I'd love to see stuff like that sometime—that sounds totally wild!"

It was Bronwyn's old friend Ginny on the phone. They'd been undergrads together in English at San Jose State. Upon graduating, however, Ginny had gone the exact opposite way of her classmate: getting married, spawning three children, spreading out at the hips, and becoming an elementary school teacher. Now Ginny and her family had just moved to a model home community called Sunset Hill Springs, and as far as Bronwyn could tell, were wildly happy.

Unlike Bronwyn. But to hear Ginny tell it, this morning at least, it was Bronwyn's life that was thrilling.

"Did you meet any celebrities at the party?" Ginny persisted.

Bronwyn felt a stab of revulsion.

"Of course not! I told you—it was a completely terrible experience."

"None?" Ginny wheedled.

"Well," Bronwyn continued unhappily, "I did talk to this woman Petra and her husband, Harold ... King or something."

To her shock, Ginny knew all about them.

"Harold *King*? He's famous! He had a spot on *Baywatch* connected with this Special Olympics program they did."

"But Ginny," Bronwyn laughed, amazed. "How do you *know* this?"

"Oh I don't know. I read about it in the *Star* or something."

The reason for Ginny's call was actually not to debrief the *LA LA* magazine party, but to invite Bronwyn to another one. "Colin Martin—do you remember him?" she asked.

"From San Jose State? *That* Colin?" Bronwyn asked.

"He called last night. He's just bought a house in L.A., is having a housewarming party ... and wants you to come."

"Oh God," Bronwyn sighed. "Do I have to?"

Colin Martin had always been the shy guy in school, nice but dull, a history major leaning toward prelaw. Large and awkward, with too-bushy eyebrows, plaid cardigans, and no chin, he was a bit of a nerd. At least, he was considered so by the lively artistic crowd Bronwyn and Paul had always been king and queen of, at their funky brown bungalow on Oak Street ...

Oak Street—*that* brought back memories. What a scene their college lives used to be! Their little cottage was always swaying, every weekend it seemed, with the sounds of the Eagles and huge gallon jugs of wine and excited conversation—their classmates, all tousled hair and Burgundy-flushed cheeks, pouring out onto the porch, the balcony, the rickety back steps leading into the tiny overgrown backyard, everything starry above, the lopsided pink flamingo whose belly everyone always rubbed, hilariously, for luck at the center of it all.

Now *that* was how to throw a party, Bronwyn reflected. Something small and intimate and family-like, everyone knowing one another's name. Everyone was the star of his own show, on Oak Street. You could talk and giggle and sing a Temptations song and just be silly—and you could hear yourself doing so.

Not like in L.A., where the shadow of celebrities or bouncers or Madonna was always hanging over you like death, the house music pumping so loud in your ears, everything so dark around you, that you felt less like a person and more like an atom or a molecule in a nuclear reactor.

"I didn't tell Colin you were still with Paul," Ginny added meaningfully. "Thought I'd leave that up to you."

"Oh God. I'd forgotten about that."

"Remember the time when Colin showed up at your birthday party in that striped flannel shirt that looked like something you'd wear over long underwear? And Paul said, 'Is that a shirt or a mattress?' He used to be so mean to him!"

"Oh dear," Bronwyn sighed. Of course, that was during Paul's hilarious twenty-one-year-old days when he slicked his hair back, wore leather jackets, rode a motorcycle, and seemed to float above everything, amused, sardonic—Youth personified. "Paul is much nicer now, Ginny. Really."

"It seemed Colin would take anything just to be near you guys. Especially you, Bronwyn. He was always so in awe of you, with your batik skirts and your incense. The exotic lit major."

"Hardly," Bronwyn snorted, but couldn't help feeling a waft of her old glamour. Colin was always such a helpless puppy. Which was why she'd always gone out of her way to be nice to him. "Some of your writing reminds me of Kera-ook," he'd said to her once. "What?" "Kera—" "Oh . . . *Kerouac*," she'd kindly corrected, touching him lightly on the arm to soften the blow.

"I think Colin still has a crush on you," Ginny teased.

"Oh pshaw," Bronwyn said, "but I'll call him anyway."

In a way it was true, though: compared with their old college buddies in San Jose, she and Paul *were* sophisticates.

And upon hanging up, Bronwyn felt the first milky gray light of comfort break over her morning. Never mind that the *LA LA* magazine party was a bust, as were many such L.A. experiences. The fact was, she and Paul did *survive* such events. And lived to tell the tale, grisly though it was. One day they would look back and laugh about all of this.

Indeed, she could picture herself and Paul entertaining in Connecticut, in a wonderful old farmhouse with warm green banker's lamps and mahogany bookshelves . . .

"Yes, those were in our dreadful L.A. days," Paul would chuckle, as the dinner party pumped him, thrillingly, for another anecdote about the terrible smoggy deadlands. Paul would lean against the wall—the "wainscoting," maybe—a little older, a little wiser, ever more handsome, chest more filled out, now that he was finally the great literary figure he was always meant to be. With his salt-and-pepper hair and tweed jacket, Paul would be looking, in fact, much like the book jacket photo on his *N.Y. Times* bestseller—a hilarious despairing novel about how terrible and shallow all the people were in L.A.

Poor Colin, Bronwyn thought again later, as she checked her mailbox at the Women's Studies department. How sad that he was actually committing himself to L.A. . . .

L.A.: the city devoid of charm, its freeways gray, its architecture a mishmash of Tudor mansions next to Art Deco faux palaces next to Spanish-style haciendas next to Alpine chalets. L.A.: the jungle of horrors. The smog-enveloped grid of everything graceless and senseless.

She could only imagine this new house he'd bought himself. Knowing Colin "Miller's Outpost" Martin, it would be the very pinnacle of convention—a cookie-cutter condo, something accounting majors bought straight out of school. She imagined powder-blue carpets, heavy oak ball furniture from Sears, a fussy cut-glass chandelier, the very talisman of the bourgeoisie. On the walnut sideboard, a ship in a bottle. When a wife called Sheila came and then two squalling children, perhaps the leatherbound set of *Encyclopaedia Britannica*—

At least she and Paul had not become that. At least they had not become that. Tujunga was not great, but at least it was not ordinary. Conventional. Middle-class.

"Good . . . morning!" Eunice, the department secretary, called out, her big white arms clutching an armload of xerox paper, long brown hair flowing behind her.

Bronwyn jumped.

"Shirley wanted to know if you could drop by this morning," Eunice said.

"Shirley? Shirley's in today?" Shirley Kent was her graduate adviser on her thesis: "Colonial American Women in Transition."

"Co-rrect. She's waiting for you in her office. Hey, cute earrings. I like those."

Well, good. Today would be the day to cinch the Connecticut offer. To stress to Shirley Kent how ready she was to take it.

"Dr. Kent?" Bronwyn pushed open the door.

"Bronwyn," Shirley Kent greeted her, flicking tired faculty adviser eyes her way. Shirley Kent did not rise from her desk, which was covered with stacks of papers and books and manuscripts, like the many high-rises of a small city. "Sit down, sit down."

Shirley Kent was a heavyset, slightly unkempt woman in her fifties. No makeup, fluffy black and gray hair pinned up casually, a rust-colored turtleneck sweater. Shirley Kent always struck Bronwyn as an old Valkyrie. Bronwyn had seen a book once—*Angry Women from the '70s*—in which Shirley Kent appeared as a much younger woman, a college activist, warlike, vengeful. Now Shirley just liked to hide in her study and read her books. All right then: a retired Valkyrie.

"How are you?" Shirley asked, distracted.

"Fine," Bronwyn assured her. "Been busy on the thesis, reading, reading, reading . . ." Although as she said those words a trace of weariness wafted over her.

"Hm." Shirley leaned her troubled face and falling-down hair back against her high-backed chair, putting her feet up on the one corner of the desk that had empty space on it. The heels of her tasseled loafers were worn down. God. Just how much does she make? Bronwyn wondered suddenly. After—what?—twenty-five years in academia?

"I wanted to tell you that I am leaving early for my sabbatical," Shirley declared, "to Connecticut. At Westbury College."

"You've been wanting to get started on that, haven't you?"

Bronwyn launched in. "To research your book on the Puritans? Which sounds fascinating—"

"Oh yes. The Marguerite Greenhill Library is really where I should be working. They have the largest and most important collection of Cotton Mather's letters on Calvinism. As well as the original manuscripts of . . ."

Bronwyn let Shirley chat on as usual. It was one of Shirley's few pleasures. Ultimately, Bronwyn was lucky to have Shirley Kent as an adviser. It could be so much worse. Hannah Levitow, for instance, in comp lit—boy did she crack the whip. Her grad students were pounding out papers and reviewing books and flying to conferences right and left. Of course, Hannah Levitow did all the hot topics, Simone de Beauvoir, Anaïs Nin, Colette. All the hotheads in women's lit wanted to do them.

Bronwyn's field—Colonial American women poets—was wide open, by comparison. No one else seemed interested. Which was why Bronwyn was attracted to them—she always was to the abandoned ones, the underdogs.

"What I thought would be exciting, then, would be for me to do a revisionist's view of Perry Miller's work on the Puritans," Shirley Kent went on, as she stirred her mug of herbal tea. "Or, I should say, a *feminist* view if I can still use the . . ."

Bronwyn's thesis, "Colonial American Women in Transition," though, had proved to be tough going. For one thing, there were so few of them. For another, what figures there were—Anne Bradstreet, Sarah Kemble Knight, some woman called Jane Ann Williams who had written just a few letters—had not produced all that much.

Not that the Colonial women poets should be blamed for their paucity of output. Those first few winters in Plymouth had been horrible. To hear the women tell it, just hammering together a wooden table made one so exhausted one had to sit down. Completing a batch of decent pickles was viewed as a major achievement. As a result, not much energy had been left over for linguistic invention. Mostly God was praised, in neat rhyming couplets, as well as spring, in all its attendant metaphors—the lutes, the merry birds, everything hopping and beribboned . . .

So some mean-spirited male critics had called such poems minor, cliché—Kmart Spenser, Keats, Donne. Well, what was wrong with using a familiar metaphor or two? Bronwyn always hotly argued. Surely, to the Colonial American women poets, such borrowed metaphors were the only familiar, tried-and-true, fail-safe mechanisms in a landscape terrifying with bears and Indians and faulty butter churns and—

When she argued, that is. Recently, it had all given her this heavy feeling.

"Anyway, I don't want to leave you in the lurch." Shirley was now hunching forward, clearly unable to shake the feeling that she *was*. "You have spring semester to write, of course. You can send me chapters as you go along. But you need to start thinking about next fall."

"As a matter of fact—" Bronwyn began.

"Starting fall '91, your Women's Studies fellowship is no longer going to be funded by the university," Shirley finally admitted, the cat out of the bag.

"What?" Bronwyn felt her heart drop to her shoes.

"Which is not to say," Shirley rushed in, "that you can't continue here. Jeffrey Hillman in English can take over as your adviser—I'm sending one or two other students his way. He's young but very good. He just did this fascinating book on *The Captivity and Restoration of Mrs. Mary Rowlandson*. And in fact, I'm sure you have a very good shot at applying to some of these other grants or fellowships or TA-ships . . ."

At that, just the slightest hint of doubt crept into Shirley Kent's voice.

Shirley Kent bit her lip. She cocked her head to one side as she riffled through the stack of applications. "How about this one? The Louella H. Annenberg Foundation Fellowship. For applicants pursuing advanced studies in women's arts and literature. Highest priority is given to . . . oh. No. Never mind."

"What I thought I could be doing in the fall," Bronwyn rallied, trying to make her voice sound stronger than she felt, "is starting at Westbury College. In that teaching position you mentioned a few months ago. At the New School."

"The New School?" Shirley Kent asked.

Bronwyn quelled the rising bubble of doubt within her.

"Yes. The New School for Alternative—"

"Bronwyn." Shirley Kent leaned forward. Her tone became stern. "The New School is focusing on *Minority* studies. *Minority* studies. African-American. Asian-American—"

Bronwyn was bewildered.

"But I thought they were going to have this huge program in seventeenth- and eighteenth-century English literature, with an emphasis on the Colonies."

"Bronwyn, the post you're talking about is going to be filled by a *Native American scholar. Native American.*"

"Native American?" The thought stunned her. Her question came out all wrong and scrambled. "Did the Indians . . . even have English literature?"

Shirley Kent put her hand on Bronwyn's arm. The hand was old, worn, gnarled, not a mother's hand but an old soldier's.

"Bronwyn. Just between you and me. My era was the seventies. It took everything we had to fight for women's rights. We fought for funding. We fought for jobs. We fought for everything. But now that pie is shrinking. All that goodwill is shifting over to minority rights. Which we've always been for, of course. But now they're pitting us against each other. In three years, UCLA may not even have a Women's Studies department."

"What?" Bronwyn felt her mind a blank.

Shirley shook her fuzzy gray and black hair from side to side. "They're taking all our funding. They're taking all our funding. There's no more money for us. No more money for us. I'm telling you, Bronwyn . . ."

For the first time Dr. Shirley Kent's tired eyes flashed. She hunched forward, her rust-colored turtleneck crumpling over the desk. She looked over her shoulder, as though her office was being bugged. And then she clutched, white-knuckled, at Bronwyn's hand, as she imparted her terrible secret.

"It's the ethnics against the women!" she whispered.

house beautiful

Bronwyn tugged at the VW bus's bad clutch, trying to get it to go into reverse. It wouldn't. It wouldn't. Come on.

With one final, kidney-splitting yank, she forced the clutch back into gear and pulled out onto Hilgard, guiding the VW into Westwood, whose once cheerful-looking boulevards looked hunched and beaten on this almost garishly sunny day. Too hot. Too hot. She struggled with the VW window crank, which was perennially stuck. Eventually the window shuddered down, squeaking.

Whew. The comforting movement of air on her face. In the background, NPR murmured:

"Economist Clare Evans calls Los Angeles a kind of world port for the twenty-first century. New companies are coming in from all over the world—Japan, the Middle East, Russia. By the year 2000 . . ."

Never mind the Westbury, Connecticut, thing. Never mind—for the moment at least—that they were imprisoned in L.A., with its traffic, its filth, its noise.

Shirley Kent's news had an even more dire, urgent cast to it: in five months her checks would stop.

This was a completely unexpected turn of events.

Bronwyn felt stunned by it, dullish.

Like an automaton, she began to calculate. Her monthly check until at least June: $1,153 after taxes. Paul's unemployment, which he would certainly get, $739. (Sigh. After what he'd been making, even unemployment looked good. Had it come to this? That she could figure in Paul's *unemployment* checks so dispassionately, without—without cringing?)

Maybe she could reapply for another one of those fellowships. True, she hadn't applied for anything in four years—her Women's Studies fellowship had been automatically renewed from year to year, she just had to fill out a form. But surely she deserved a grant as much as the next person. And then, if she really put her mind to it, maybe she could whip this Ph.D. thing together by, say, fall of '92, maybe publish a paper, begin applying for assistant professorships . . .

Dr. Shirley Kent's tasseled loafers with the worn-down heels floated before her.

How had it come to happen, Bronwyn suddenly thought, that her life was filled with all this worn-downness, this scuffing, this wrinkling, this sagging?

Why—look at the . . . the peeling plastic, the torn seat covers of the VW bus. She had always loved it—what it represented, their funkiness and their freedom—but they really had to fix it up. Get new seat covers. Maybe Mexican stripe, from the Four Winds Emporium, something cheerful . . .

She turned to look at it.

On the back seat were the bags Bronwyn had neatly tied

together of recycling stuff—plastic, paper, aluminum. On the floor were two cardboard boxes of old clothes she was planning to take to an L.A. Children's Mission benefit the Women's Studies program was sponsoring. Way in the back was an old electric fan they were going to lend to an actor friend of theirs in Venice.

So many good deeds had been done in this VW bus.

But at this moment, the bus looked positively worn, overladen, battered by good intentions. At this moment, it was hard to say who really needed the help.

Come to think of it, Shirley Kent drove a somewhat bedraggled car as well. Bronwyn had seen it, one day, when they'd walked to the faculty parking lot. It was some kind of Audi from, well, from the seventies, practically. With a cracked dashboard. And gray terrier hair all over a blanket cover on the back seat.

Her glance fell over her own passenger's seat, which cradled Colin's gift. Tch. To bless Colin's home, she'd decided to bring him a brass Thai miniature-elephant planter she had gotten once at the Four Winds Emporium during a big sale. Actually, in her excitement, she had gotten six of them. "But what are you going to do with all those?" Paul had asked. "Five dollars!" was all she could cry out, falteringly. "They were only five dollars!"

To staid Colin Martin, she knew, the brass elephant would seem exotic and artistic . . . but the thought gave her little pleasure now. She'd rather not have to visit him today—to drive all the way out to hot, smoggy Pasadena, land of blue-haired women, to see dull old annoying Colin and his dull old house. She had never been to Pasadena, but imagined it like the Valley: a merciless grid of tract homes and strip malls, aching under a brown sky.

When she got to the freeway, it was throbbing with hostility, angry sun reflecting off whizzing metal and windshields, the air soured with farts of exhaust. How can we stay in this city? she wondered. The graffiti, the trash, the smog: Ugly, ugly, ugly, ugly! Hot, hot, hot, hot!

But when she swung the shuddering VW onto Arroyo Parkway thirty minutes later, it dawned on her that Pasadena was surprisingly pretty. It was not like the hideous senseless jumble of L.A. at all.

She turned up California Boulevard. California Boulevard—how lovely.

There were magnolia trees everywhere, lush lawns, shiny Volvos—new ones, '90 ones—parked in the shade. Up above, the sun dappled through ever-spreading canopies of branches; the occasional leaf dropped and fluttered over the new black asphalt. As she turned, slowing, onto Colin's street—Oakdale—a blond ten-year-old in a neat backpack jingled his bike bell as he rode by, sucking on a lollipop. The halting cadences of someone working their way through a Bach piano étude floated across the air. A plump white cat lolled contentedly under a geranium bush. "Ohhh," she exhaled. Her breath caught in her throat.

The scene reminded her of something ineffable . . . her childhood . . . the suburbs . . .

San Jose, California . . .

This incredible longing and sadness . . .

"Where am I going in my life?" she sighed, picking up her brass elephant planter with its brave blue bow. "Where am I going?"

She rang the bell.

The white door, framed by pine-green trim, opened.

But it was the wrong house. Because the man who opened the door was . . .

Six-foot-three. Broad-chested. Light eyes. Rugged chin. Blue oxford shirt. Light brown hairs curling up toward the neck. Kind of like a hunky blond Bruce Jenner.

She laughed nervously and spun on her heel to go: "Oh, I'm sorry. I—"

"Bronwyn?"

"Colin?"

Her voice was a whisper of terror.

"It's so good to see you," Colin Martin said, a little shyly. He leaned forward to enfold her in an embrace. Crisp linen. Nice smell. Muscle. Jesus! Bronwyn felt tiny in his arms.

Colin held her at arm's length, and looked at her. "Bronwyn! Are you okay?"

"Oh yes, yes," she said. "It's just been a—long day. Long day. And such a long time since I've seen you! You look terrific! Congratulations! Ginny said . . ." From somewhere deep within herself, she found her chatter, launched into it.

It was the chin. As a law student, Colin had never had a chin. He was all nose. But sometime in the last seven years this definite *chin* had jutted forward on Colin's face. And suddenly everything—the gray eyes, the straight, once too-bushy eyebrows, the wide mouth—yanked into perfect proportion. There was a jawline, the skin had cleared and turned a light bronze, the torso had fleshed out, and this—this Man had appeared.

"Here you go," she fluttered, handing him the little brass elephant planter. "From an exotic—not really—" she amended, self-deprecatingly, but she hoped not annoyingly so, "literature major."

"Awww," he said, cocking his head as he looked at it, almost as though masking puzzlement. Well, well, well—underneath he was still the same funny old Colin after all. "That's nice. That's nice.

Well: I'll put it in the garden. All right. Yes. That's what I'll do. Thanks!"

"Well, isn't this nice?" she said cautiously, giving a cursory glance to the front entryway with its domed ceiling and Spanish tile. She put up her hands. "Congratulations!"

"It's so nice of you to make the time to come by," he said, a bit formal.

"Time? Of course, Colin, you know I always would for you. And this is so . . . so lovely," she said, ever polite.

"Well: the house is a little on the old-fashioned side. It was built in 1934. But as you know, I've always been distressingly conservative. Always so staid next to you wild Bohemians."

"Oh not at all." Bronwyn was embarrassed to be reminded of how they used to mock him. "Would you . . . like to give me a tour?"

In fact, Colin Martin's house was not nearly as horrible as she thought it would be.

His living room was light and airy, with actually rather nice period accents like built-in wooden bookcases, a cove ceiling, and lily-shaped wall sconces.

"I'm sure I'm never going to run this thing," Colin said, shaking his head, drawing the two wire-mesh curtains shut on his used-brick fireplace. "A fireplace—in Southern California! What were these people thinking?"

"It's wonderful!" Bronwyn assured him. "What a lovely thing to have."

"It's been so crazy for me these last couple of years, I've completely lost touch with what everyone's been doing. I didn't even know that you were in L.A. What's been going on with you?"

Bronwyn opened her mouth to speak, but felt a wave of exhaustion come over her.

"Listen, Colin." She turned to him, put her hand on his arm. "Let's have this be your day, okay? Why don't we start with you? Are you still with that law firm? MacKenzie and . . ."

"Actually"—he raised his eyebrows, matter-of-factly—"I'm with ABC now."

"ABC? Really? In the legal department?"

"Actually"—he reached over to open a curtain—"I'm in Dramatic Series Development. Kind of the vice president of."

"Good for you. But how did you make that transition?"

"It's interesting. After getting my law degree, I decided to take a year off. Just on a whim, I decided to take this intern job in the mailroom at Lorimar. I was lucky enough to meet a guy named Jim Harroldson, who kind of took me under his wing. He had been at William Morris for a while in . . ."

They pressed forward to the dining room.

This gave Bronwyn pause. So he had an actual formal dining room. With dark paneling and a—a stained-glass window depicting some kind of colored bird in flight. Through the surrounding clear panes she could see rosebushes, delicate, fragrant, not a spot on them. They were as perfect, as manicured, as sleek as—as Petra King's pageboy haircut.

"Television, of course, has its drawbacks. It's so hard to get good stuff done. The quality of the writers is just so low. There's like a shallow bench of . . ."

Ahead was an arched hallway. And—and a staircase. Heavens to Betsy, this house seemed to go on and on. There would be roommates, no doubt, to help him with the mortgage . . .

"Was this—was this house really expensive?" Bronwyn asked timidly. "How do you afford all of this?"

Colin stopped for a moment, as though caught in the act of something.

"Well, they don't pay us peanuts at ABC of course. But the bottom line is, I guess I just got lucky with the move-up market," Colin admitted finally, shrugging his huge shoulders in a winsome, faintly chagrined way.

"The move-up market?" Bronwyn asked, tilting her head out the window. Was that a . . . three-car garage? And redwood deck leading to . . .

"I don't know if you remember, but I bought this condo in West L.A. in '84? Wasn't much to look at. No patio. Ugly carpeting. Kind of a cheesy bachelor pad, really."

"Oh I'm sure it wasn't that bad," Bronwyn mumbled. And a spa and gazebo? Was that a spa and gazebo in back?

"The thing is . . ." Colin leaned forward, earnest, imparting serious information to her. "I bought that condo for fifty-three thousand dollars. I put some nice wallpapering in, updated some fixtures—you know, faucets, the tub. And you know what I sold it for, just five years later?"

Bronwyn shook her head dumbly.

"A hundred and seventy-nine thousand!"

"A hundred and seventy-nine?" The number hit her like a blow.

Colin had a shyly guilty expression on his face, as though he were saying "Yikes!" "I cleared almost a hundred and thirty thousand! Tax-free, due to the rollover. And boom: I had the down payment for this house which is, well, a little bigger. It was that easy." He shook his head. "It's this market, I tell you. Southern

California has gone crazy. I had four offers on my condo! It's this constant influx of people into L.A."

"The influx," Bronwyn repeated, pushing forward through a polished wooden door. His words floated after her.

"L.A. has become this world port, this magnet. They're coming in from all over the world—Japan, the Middle East, Russia. By the year 2000, real estate here is going to be more precious than gold. Particularly right *in* the city, the closer in, the better. Because there's nowhere to expand. There's no more space. It's like this dense nucleus . . ."

Then she saw his kitchen.

Colin Martin's kitchen was the most perfect thing she'd ever seen.

In a single stroke, it transcended time, space, scuffed-shoeness, battered carness, wrinkled-jacketness, lapsed-promiseness, decay.

She could almost hear a choir of angels.

Silvery light fell through wide skylights onto brightly polished hanging copper pans. Surrounding Bronwyn on four sides was a sea of blue-and-white-checked tile, fresh as a New England morning.

New England. Martha's Vineyard. Connecticut . . .

She had never been to these wondrous lands, of course, but she knew them from her fantasies—she had a keen sense of their perennial dewiness, the heady cut of their salt breezes.

Ahead of her was a large square garden window in which leafy green herbs opened and twisted.

In the center of the room, altarlike, stood a solid, golden, country butcher-block table. Resting in one corner was a set of gleaming German carving knives. Colin had been chopping parsley, onions, yellow peppers, tomatoes—the ruby red slices fanned out to the right, elegant as a line of poetry. On the far side of it, a sink . . . Was it?

Yes.

"Corian," read the letters discreetly etched near the faucets.

"Corian," Bronwyn whispered. So Grecian, so pristine. She reached out her forefinger and touched it. "Corian," she repeated, feeling a swell of longing so great she couldn't stop the trembling.

"UCLA. I'm at UCLA right now," Bronwyn murmured in a trance. "Women's lit. Colonial American women's poetry."

She had tried to leave, but as the hour ticked by, she'd somehow found herself frozen in that kitchen, even as the images of Colin's housewarming party swirled before her in a sickening dream.

"Oh really?" The woman she was conversing with had short, dyed-black, vaguely dandruffy hair, topped with a beret. A beret. "I am really, really arty!" it screamed. Her lipstick was the wrong color. Her purplish scarf seemed soiled. She had only one, slashingly geometrical earring on and she seemed a bit flustered about it. Crow's-feet grouped around her eyes. What was she—in her late thirties? This woman had been in the arts too long. She had had too many meatless meals and cigarettes and espresso. She had slept on so many futons she was developing a permanent hunchback.

Slightly beyond them, in the nerve center of the party, all of Colin's sleek, khakied friends were washing in in waves, bearing bottles of wine and congratulations and hugs and all of that Hollywood bla bla bla bla. "Did you hear about the NBC bla bla bla bla bla? And that Warren Littlefield bla bla bla bla?" On either side of Colin, helping him take the gifts and coats, were two dewy, lean-hipped, swinging-long-haired, intern-on-the-rise-looking twenty-three-year-olds positively radiating a certain brisk, alert, laughing energy.

An energy that, Bronwyn realized, she had once had. As in past tense.

"Thank you, Anders." The brunette smiled, her smile lines barely creasing her soft downy cheeks. She leaned forward to accept an air kiss from a bearded fortyish man, bending one knee and gracefully pointing up one $80 Joan & David shoe behind her, revealing its varnished bottom. Even the sole of her shoe was shiny, Bronwyn noticed—the *sole* of her *shoe*.

Beyond that, on the used-brick patio, were the housewarming goodies, a tumble of gift bags with their embossed names: Conran's Habitat, Williams-Sonoma, Crate & Barrel. Toppled over on one side, Bronwyn's once cute little $5 brass elephant planter from the Four Winds Emporium looked puny and bereft and even seemed to be developing a few weird mold spots next to the smooth-cheeked, symmetrically placed terra-cotta vases that fringed Colin's manicured back lawn like sentries. Sentries of perfect Eurotaste. And money.

"I love your earrings," the one-earring Bohemian was saying. "Have you heard of this place called the Four Winds Emporium? It's really, really great. You can get stuff like that for, like, four dollars. In the bargain bin section."

Bronwyn looked at the woman in horror.

"You go to the Four Winds?"

"Oh yeah, all the time. That's where I got this scarf." She gestured to her awful wrinkled little scarf. "But now I've decided to start designing my *own* jewelry."

"Great," Bronwyn said.

"And hats," the women said. "I love hats. Speaking of hats, I was really hoping to meet Petra King today."

"Petra King . . ." Bronwyn started to respond, but trailed off. The only conversational item Bronwyn could offer was that she had once tried to schmooze Petra King—and failed. So Bronwyn merely shrugged her shoulders and took another sad sip of her white wine—fluted stemware, Charter Hill Chardonnay, perfectly chilled: $17.99 a bottle. There were bottles and bottles in the perfect refrigerator.

"Have you heard of her? She's married to Harold King, you know, the film guy? Petra King designs jewelry. I would love to have her look at my designs." Beret Woman's face appeared to look at the future, and it frightened her. "If I could just get a marketer! Or a publicist! It's so frustrating."

"What's frustrating?" Colin appeared behind the beret, his hands lifting two glasses of wine from the counter. His eyes met Bronwyn's. "Hey. Are you okay? You've barely left your post all afternoon."

"I'm fine," Bronwyn whispered, lifting her glass.

"Petra King," the Bohemian repeated, clearly off on her own obsession, chanting her own mantra. "Colin, what time did she say she might be showing up?"

Colin looked at his watch, something vaguely nautical with wheels and dials. When he looked up, his face was blank. Even gentle. "Chelsea, I'm actually not even sure she and Harold are in town right now."

"Oh they *are,* but you would never catch Petra dead in *Pasadena.*"

Everyone turned in the direction of the voice. It came from a tall, slim black woman in red, green, yellow, and black coveralls and army boots. With her dreadlocks and slitty sunglasses, she looked like she had just stepped out of some MTV video. Or like an oracle of some kind. She put her slim brown hand, jangly with bracelets, on Colin's.

"Nothing personal, man, but Petra doesn't come this far east."

Colin shook his head and laughed, a bit baleful. "You see, Bronwyn, I told you I was distressingly conservative. And obviously too much so for some people."

The MTV person ticked off the locations on her hands.

"Petra doesn't like to come east of the 101. She was saying all this on a shoot we were doing a couple of months ago. Glendale? Pasadena? Forget it. And she won't go north of Studio City—Ventura Boulevard is the cutoff for her in the Valley."

"Well, *no one* goes to the Valley," Chelsea declared supportively. She was nodding her head doggedly as MTV spoke, as though committing this important geographical information about Petra King to memory. It was as though each bounce of her dyed-black head jogged her brain into a new, better configuration, lodging Petra's opinions firmly in place of her own.

"Not even I would live in the Valley," Colin put in gamely.

"What does Petra King think of Echo Park?" Chelsea asked nervously. "I was thinking of moving there. It's pretty cool, actually—it's got a lot of little coffee shops and poetry readings and—and hills and—"

"Grimy," MTV declared. "I think that's the word she used. Yep. Grimy. Echo Park is 'grimy.' "

"Jeez." Chelsea looked beaten. "How about Silverlake? Of course, Silverlake is totally beyond my price range!" She turned and addressed this to Bronwyn, who she somehow had zeroed in on as her equally disadvantaged companion, her fellow wrinkled Bohemian in this frightening new Crate & Barrel world.

"And she won't ever go below the 10," MTV rolled on, snapping her gum. "Occasionally she'll do Venice, but that's about the exception. She's real finicky about her driving. She doesn't like certain freeways. She won't come certain places. That chick is out."

L.A., Bronwyn thought sadly.

A town without a center.

Not that she cared that L.A. had no center, no one place that everyone would drive to.

Nor did she care that she and Paul lived in Tujunga. Sunland. Off the 118. So far away it was not even attached to the 101—or to any of the freeways these people were talking about.

She did not even care that Colin lived here magnificently alone, sans roommates, that upstairs he had an airy study with hardwood floors and even a—a library, and a master bathroom with wonderful old tile and a clawfoot tub from England and a marble-pedestal (Kohler) sink.

But what she did care about was this kitchen. This vision of freshness. The skylights, the hanging copper pans, the dappled garden windows, the blue and white tile, the peerless butcher block with its graceful fan of tomato slices. She was instinctively drawn to it, with the fierceness a mother lion feels for her cub. This kitchen was a sign, a totem, a set piece from another universe . . . another life entirely—*the life she should be living*.

When was it—exactly when was the moment in their lives she

and Paul had said no to all this? What was the wrong turn they had taken, the turn that led to linoleum and Formica and desperation and squalor and uncertainty and exile and failure . . .

She closed her eyes, and found herself physically hanging on to this room, stroking its tile, warming herself in its skylights.

hoffstead

incorporated

When NPR clicked on that morning at eight—"From Washington, I'm Mara Liasson"—Bronwyn Peters broke into a scream.

My God, she thought, hurtling upward toward consciousness. Why am I screaming?

But she didn't even have to open her eyes to see the rock-hard futon, the battered Kaypro computer, the brown swing-arm lamp like a buzzard . . .

So different from the dream she had been having.

In the dream, she had watched herself float into her and Paul's bathroom (gray linoleum, yellow plastic flowers on shower curtain, rusty aluminum faucet). By the light of a candle, the bathwater running, she calmly sat down on the toilet seat and began to pore lovingly over the latest issues of *House & Garden, Better Homes and Gardens: Remodeling Ideas, Martha Stewart Living*. She kissed the glossy pages—the flawless butcher-block islands, Sub-Zero refrigerators, tracklit highboys, cut-glass backsplashes, Italian ceramic serving plates.

But then Paul's voice sounded outside the door: "Noni? What are you doing in there?"

"Nothing! Just taking a long bath!" she called out, frantically stuffing the magazines behind the toilet.

But the door burst open, and Paul sprang in. With unerring instinct, he immediately found the magazines. He waved them in the air at her—as stung as if he'd found a dog-eared issue of *Playgirl*.

"Kitchens, kitchens, kitchens!" he cried out. "Cape Cod make-overs! My God! Look at these photographs! Don't you know that homes like this don't really exist? They use special angles—airbrushing!"

"Maybe if we didn't live in Tujunga," she flashed back at him, "I wouldn't have to *look* at magazines!"

At just that moment, as if to push the point home, the pulsing disco beat of Frankie Goes to Hollywood blatted out from the living room, bringing her back to dismal reality.

"No-o-o-o-o-o!" Bronwyn moaned, as the beat pulsed on. "No-o-o-o-o-o!"

"What—" Paul flew into the room. "Noni! Are you okay?"

Bronwyn felt her customary despair sweeping back upon her.

At that moment, what she wanted to tell Paul was: "I'm leaving this house, or I'm leaving you. I can't go on in this chaos! I'm at the end of my rope!" And more.

But on seeing the tired, anxious face of her beloved—the serious gray eyes, the wide twisting mouth—she couldn't.

What came out instead was: "Would it be too much for Jonathan to play Mozart on Sunday mornings? What's with him? If he hates gays so much, why does he always play gay disco music? And what about his rent? We're ten days past due. George Ko-foupoulous is going to evict us if—"

"Jonathan gave me a check this morning."

"What?"

Bronwyn couldn't believe her ears.

No. This didn't happen . . . never happened in daylight. Never in this universe.

Paul opened a drawer of the bureau and lifted out the magical slip of paper. He walked to her seductively, smiling. By some trick of the morning light, he actually looked slightly less hunched, more straightened out, more assured than usual. Even a bit of a mischievous side-to-side lilt seemed to be animating the draw-string of his Four Winds karate pants.

"How—how much?" Bronwyn whispered.

"He paid off that last half of last month's that he was behind on and all of this month's. He even"—Paul slid down next to her—"put in toward half of next month's DWP bill!"

"No!" she crowed in delight. But indeed, there it was: $487.36, scrawled in Jonathan's quick officious hand. In the "Memo" section, importantly, were listed all of the brave little check's accomplishments ("Last mo's rent, ½—This mo's rent," etc.). That was Jonathan's way—no check from him in three months and then suddenly it was as though he were a persnickety student demanding an A+ for effort.

While they had been expecting, hoping, to get that money eventually, if in dribs and drabs—$75 here, $120 there—getting it all at once, in a single check, was a rush, a real rush.

Bronwyn felt the receipt of the money as an almost physical sensation, a little wool padding against the cold winter of despair, a temporary plug in her sinking boat.

"I thought we had kissed that sixty-two thirty-six good-bye! I thought his unemployment had run out! I thought—"

Paul put his arm around her, laid his cheek against hers. "Jonathan made a sale."

"Thank God," she breathed, burying her nose in his hair. "Thank God he's gone back to selling pot!"

"Wasn't pot," Paul corrected, pulling his arm back, stroking her cheek.

"Mushrooms!" she exclaimed, squeezing his hand.

Growing mushrooms had been one of the many projects Jonathan had undertaken in his closet in the last few months—aside from what they considered his ongoing biological experiments with mildewy sweatshirts, rancid sneakers, and seeing how much cat hair could accumulate in one place. For some reason, Jonathan's fat and angry cat, Velvet, made her lurking place his dreadful closet, from which wrinkled laundry spilled, unmoved for months at a time. "Who knows what's in that closet?" Bronwyn always joked to Paul, and they would both go "Oooooh!" in mock fright.

Building on the theme of fetidity, recently Jonathan had ordered away to some unnamed Boulder company for a mini-hydroponics setup kit you could assemble yourself. It was by far the most beautiful object in the house, a hexagonal white prism of shining plastic and Lucite, with ducts for air and water and a base at the bottom for laying down soil.

Bronwyn and Paul had wondered at the possible cost of the hydroponics setup. After all, those could be precious checking account dollars Jonathan was sapping from shared costs like the rent and the phone bill. (Not to mention household goods like Pine-Sol. "Don't you think he should pitch in for the Pine-Sol?"

Bronwyn had wondered. "It costs almost five dollars a bottle—
and I buy it every two months." "Then again it's not like he uses
it," Paul retorted. "Jonathan's bathroom! Ooh!" they said, shivering.)

Then again, like nervous agents of a temperamental talent, they
figured they should indulge Jonathan his odd purchases. So Jonathan was thirty-three and unemployed. So no viable careers
seemed to be forming around him as his months in L.A. passed.
He *had* finished the Ph.D. after all. The French horn was a tough
instrument. At one point in his teens, he had even been considered
the brightest in the Hoffstead family. Surely he would eventually
stumble onto something.

Perhaps, then, if they made the mistake of squeezing $38 for
last month's phone bill, they would be taking away his proverbial
fishing pole and not just his fish. "We have to think about this in
the long run," Paul had said. "If he really gets this mushroom thing
going he could make a lot of money. He can sell them for thirty,
forty dollars a baggie. He knows a lot of out-of-work musicians
here in L.A.—they're his client base."

And in fact, the mushrooms Jonathan made were quite potent.
On one weekend, Bronwyn and Paul had taken some and crawled
around their house pointing out the Aztec sunburst tile and
harvest-gold shag carpeting to each other with much hilarity. Then
they went into Jonathan's bathroom and found a bottle of flea
shampoo in the tub—ostensibly for Velvet, but they could just see
Jonathan giving himself a flea bath. That was it, that was totally it.
They had collapsed against each other howling with laughter.

"The hydroponics finally paid off!" Bronwyn enthused. "Good
for him!" Frankie Goes to Hollywood still pulsed through the
door, but now she was feeling much more forgiving. The sunlight

through the half-moon of the ripped curtain shone something like a promise. A sprig of walnut leaves danced outside.

"No, it was computer stuff," Paul said. "Anyway—"

"Pot, pot," she mourned. "Why doesn't he go back to growing pot? It's the one thing he excels at! It's his calling!"

"He sold this accounting software thing to some businessman in Delaware for eight hundred dollars. Anyway, I have bigger news."

Paul leapt from the futon, barely able to contain himself.

"I—I got a job!"

"What?"

"Writing! A film!"

Bronwyn felt a surge of excitement . . .

Followed by the usual grim caution. Barometer correction. Descend. Descend.

Because how often she had heard this.

It was the curse of Los Angeles.

The meeting that was *just about* to happen. The contracts *just an hour* from being signed.

Nothing ever came through for them here in Los Angeles— this terrible basin where palm trees shimmered like mirages in the wavy heat.

But she must support him. She must support him.

"What is it?" she asked, arranging her features into a mask of hopeful enthusiasm.

"Well, it's not exactly a film," he amended. And yet he continued to pace, gleeful. "It's a video. All right. An industrial. It's an industrial."

"An industrial?"

"The point is, it shoots for ten months. And I'm making a bundle!" he crowed.

"How big a bundle?" Bronwyn's face still wore its supportive mask.

"Twenty-five thousand!" he enthused, whipping a second check out of the drawer. It was, indeed, the first installment. "Pay to the order of Paul Hoffstead," it said, "$3,500."

"Oh Paul," she breathed, embracing him, her eyes teary. She felt new light breaking over their tired bedroom. And not a harsh light but a forgiving one, bathing everything—the battered Kaypro computer, the rumpled futon, the brown swing-arm lamp—in soft focus.

Best of all, at the bottom of the scene hovered its magical caption: *"Before."* As for *"After"*? Who knew?

"But how—"

"Henry," he said, kissing her on the nose. "Remember? My old friend from school? At the *LA LA* magazine party?"

"Henry!" she bubbled, marveling. She tweaked his nose, teasing. "And you're the guy who never wants to go to parties! You're the guy who never thinks he has connections!"

"Well, L.A." He shrugged his shoulders. "I guess if you stay around here long enough, they can't ignore you forever!"

"Oh Paul, this is wonderful!"

"As farm folk say in South Dakota . . ." Here he put his hands on his hips, adopted his best Barney Fife imitation. " 'After even the coldest winter has to come the spring.' "

Farmers. Survivors. Yes. That's what they were.

She felt a palpable electric connection beginning to flow again between them.

And all at once, Bronwyn realized how long disappointment had paralyzed them, holding them prisoners in this house, sad ghosts in wrinkled sweatpants, miniature action heroes whose powers—of quick wit (Paul) and cool batik fabric (Bronwyn)—would not work on this mysterious and terrible new planet.

But deep down, lying dormant, was always the ancient sense of who they had decided to be. Paul was the artist. Bronwyn was the true heart—the one who believed in Paul. That was what she was meant to do. Either that or it was a habit she had fallen into, she didn't even know anymore. In any case, what she did know was that doubting in Paul's future—and therefore hers—made her sick to her stomach.

But now, knowing who they were again—being rerooted, their feet once again touching that continent, that vast underground continent that was Paul's Talent—they could take each other's hands again and rejoin the world.

She would make him his favorite breakfast—jalapeño, avocado, and jack cheese omelette with hot salsa and potatoes. He would rub her back, maybe braid her hair like he used to. They would make love.

Afterward, they would take the *L.A. Times* and maybe *Harper's* for Paul and drive out to Silverlake, find a table at the Onyx, pet the cats there, drink some cappuccinos. Maybe then they'd walk through the lawns of Griffith Park. Window-shop in Chinatown. Drive into Pasadena for a matinee at one of the cute new theaters. Pick up some pâté and wine later at Trader Joe's. It would be the first nice day in a very long time.

"What's the video, by the way?" she asked, as an afterthought.

"Oh . . . it's this new career management video series called *Diversity 2000 with Zibby Tanaka*."

"Diversity 2000?"

"It's . . ." Paul's face looked perturbed for just a second, then blossomed into enthusiasm. "You know how Los Angeles is becoming a melting pot of different ethnicities? This business consultant Zibby Tanaka has done a series of books on managing diversity toward the year 2000. It's pretty interesting, really."

Diversity. Multiculturalism. Ethnicities. Shirley Kent's voice floated back to her:

"I tell you, Bronwyn, it's the ethnics against the women!"

Bronwyn felt a slight stab of angst as she remembered her UCLA situation, the one she hadn't yet told Paul about . . .

On the other hand, she thought, as she padded toward the kitchen, the fact that Paul's video was on diversity was actually good. Yes.

She was totally for diversity and multiculturalism. She always had been. Just last week she had given $10 to some Chilean Poets Rights group she'd heard about on KPFK. It was about time, in the nineties, that all the underdogs had their day.

And as far as she and Paul went, if only one of them had to give up their job to an ethnic person so the wealth of employment could be spread equally, that was perfectly fine with her.

Anyway, she was realizing more and more every day what she didn't really want to be anymore: a brilliant but poorly paid scholar slaving away on the Colonial American women writers.

What she did want . . . was a home she could decorate and make all her own. And at that moment, with Paul suddenly amazingly employed, she realized it didn't even have to be in Connecticut, in Pasadena, or anywhere else.

It could be in Los Angeles. Sure. There were plenty of different neighborhoods to choose from in Los Angeles. They could find a new place to rent—still reasonable, convenient for Paul of course, but with just a little bit of charm to it. With a kitchen that wasn't irredeemably gross. It was totally possible. Given just that one thing—a hub, a center, a small oasis of unexpectedly lovely tile—she could endure anything.

Full of hope, she could even face her own kitchen today.

Its meager counter space was all done in chipped Formica, white with dull gunmetal-colored veins shot through it. The floor was orange and brown Aztec linoleum. The fridge was an avocado-green number which constantly grew icebergs within it. There were macaroni-and-cheese-stained pots left out by . . .

She could even face Jonathan today—who stood at the sink, dunking a tea bag into his favorite *Star Trek* mug, the one with Spock. The velour bathrobe had been ditched. He was, as usual, shoeless, but he had on a clean, not-too-wrinkled gray sweatshirt, and a pair of beige corduroys that looked, if not new, unfamiliar. And he had shaved. Wow! The young entrepreneur!

The sun was sure shining on the Hoffstead brothers today!

"So Jonathan . . ." Bronwyn said pleasantly. "Heard you sold something. Software. Things are going well for you, then?"

Jonathan grinned. His gray eyes shone behind his glasses. It was not a pretty sight. Jonathan had the kind of grin that always seemed to be celebrating the troubles of somebody else. His was the sort of grin that said, "I really snookered *that* guy, and how!" But today Bronwyn would celebrate that grin.

"Oh yeah," he threw out casually. "Hoffstead Software Systems is rolling. Knew it was just a matter of time . . ."

Hoffstead Software Systems. Jonathan's private corporation. Of which he was the president, the president of cat hair and smelly tennis shoes and a slimy shower stall that had never seen a scrub brush. And yet, six months ago Jonathan had blithely printed up a thousand neat business cards ($28.75—she had seen the receipt) in his niggling, A-student manner.

Bronwyn had shaken her head once, a disbeliever. But now it all seemed to be paying off.

She lifted the chipped Mr. Coffee pot from its white plastic housing, poured coffee into a mug. She wanted to turn tail and head right back into the bedroom—but Jonathan was holding his tea to his lips, silently waiting for her rejoinder.

Okay. She closed her eyes and felt the goodness, kindness, and warmth flooding back to her.

Benevolent Bronwyn: it was her better self—the person she wanted to be, liked to be, knew how to be.

"So . . ." she began again, full of patient interest. "What exactly is this software thing you invented? What does it do?"

"Come on," Jonathan said, studying her face, cynicism vying with a plaintive desire to talk about himself. "You're not really interested, are you? You're just glad I made some money finally. You're just glad I gave you guys a check."

"No, no!" Bronwyn cried out, stung to be found out, her face flaming to the roots of her hair. "Of course not!"

"You're not really interested in computers. Are you?" In spite of himself, Jonathan's voice cracked with hopefulness on his last question.

"I am, I am!" she insisted, feeling a gush of goodwill for Jonathan, poor misunderstood Jonathan who felt no one was ever interested in his stuff. "I think your work is very interesting! I think it's just—great that you can invent things and market them. What a business head! I mean," Bronwyn added expansively, "of course I'm glad about the check. I'm sure you are too. It's frustrating not having money. I'm sure you're glad yourself."

"This paying rent thing is for the birds." Jonathan scowled.

"You know how much money I threw away in rent last year? Something like twenty-five hundred bucks! Gone! What a rotten system."

"Well, unfortunately"—Bronwyn chose her words carefully— "that *is* the system until our generation can change it." She was often taken aback at how Jonathan could view himself as being the sole victim of an oppressive Other. Meanwhile she and Paul were covering $210 DWP bills with no help from him, and floating him his rent. But that was all in the past.

"What I really want to do, once I get my software company going, is to buy property. That's the way to have the system work for you instead of against. You have your tax shelter, your investment is rising in value, and you can rent out space too. That's income. It's a really good system. It's a way to build something."

"Oh I see," she said politely. She had to admit that it did resonate with things Colin had said, and therefore must have some kind of credence.

"You can do a thing where you just put a five percent payment down and you borrow even that. You pay the mortgage in rental income. There are a million ways . . ."

The details were getting away from her a little bit, but still she listened, indulging him.

In the meantime, in came Velvet, crouching on the orange and brown linoleum, her little fanged mouth opening in a kind of silent, foul-tempered cat scream. She'd somehow absorbed a black sock from Jonathan's laundry. It drooped across her back like a saddle, trailing on the ground. The lone member of the Hoffstead Software conglomerate.

Undaunted, its president calculated on. "I do need to gather just a bit of cash to pay off my Visa bill. Clean credit and all. And I have to keep Hoffstead Software going at least one more month so it looks like I have income. But after that—no problem. Uncle Sam *wants* us to buy real estate. It *helps* the economy. It's what this country was built on!"

flamingo's rest

"So . . . how are things going out there in Los Angeles?" Hub Hoffstead boomed, as he pushed open the door of the Country Squire station wagon. His raggedy white eyebrows were raised as though expecting the worst. "We read every week in the Sioux Falls paper about murders and robberies and those—what are they?"

"Drive-by shootings," Dorothy Hoffstead answered precisely, as though she'd been waiting all morning to pronounce the words. Her outfit, a medley of powder-blue polyester and beige-and-yellow plaids, matched Hub's. Over the years, their curly white coifs, always with the same degree of fouff, had become more like those of brother and sister than husband and wife.

Bronwyn sighed. This visit to Florida, for Hub and Dorothy's fiftieth wedding anniversary, held in the trailer park the Hoffsteads visited each winter, was not going to be easy.

She tilted her chin up, however. A negative attitude came from *"Before."* *"Before"* Paul had started to get four-digit checks as a director. *"Before"* Bronwyn had broken the news about the waning of her UCLA fellowship. *"Before"* Paul said that he didn't care—she should take six months off to find herself, they could afford it. *"Before"* Paul had agreed that they should start looking for a better place to rent immediately.

Paul worked so hard, his parents would give him a break, they would, Bronwyn thought. They had to—

"Robberies and drive-by shootings—that's just what they print in the papers in the Midwest," Paul was smoothly assuring Hub and Dorothy. Bronwyn marveled at the change in Paul's voice that came about when he spoke to his parents. His vocal tone took on an unnaturally smooth, burnished quality—as smooth and burnished as the calm, flat ocean he and Bronwyn supposedly sailed on. ("Life is *good*!" he'd always declare over the phone, the word "good" veering toward a hearty shout. "We're *fine*!")

"Los Angeles is like any city, you know." Paul strained to push positive energy forward toward the front of the Country Squire. "There are bad parts, and then there are *good* parts." He patted Dorothy's powder-blue polyester shoulder. That trademark shout was coming into his voice again. "We're *fine*!"

"You do know that Sioux Falls was voted the number-one city to live in in America, don't you?" Hub threw out casually, as he pulled out of the airport parking lot and onto the highway.

"Yes, Dad, you told us!" Paul exclaimed. "Too bad it's thirty below there or you'd be there right now, huh?" he added, getting a slight dig in, winking at Bronwyn.

"Well, we do like Florida in the winter," Dorothy admitted. "Never gets below about sixty-five. You get quite a few sunny days like this in California, do you?" she asked.

But she seemed uncertain the sun really shone in California, as though, perhaps, it was all advertising.

The midafternoon sun indeed shone down on the marshlands of Florida, over the two-lane highway, over palm trees and green lawns, over the many trailer parks, signs painted cheerfully as movie marquees. "Snowbird!" "Sunset Homes!" "Paradise Alley!" Winnebagos and big Ford station wagons much like Hub's roared by. Beyond the twisted telephone lines lay low brown hills, unadorned by much vegetation. "Pepsi," a billboard said.

"And work?" Dorothy turned to them. Her birdlike face, with its sharp tiny nose and alert eyes, was a mask of worry. Bronwyn felt compelled to jump in.

"Terrific about Paul's job, isn't it?" Bronwyn found that she was also shouting toward the Hoffsteads' curly white heads. "Great job—*and* really great pay! It's also the kind of thing that can lead to a lot of other things! Paul's really, really on his way now! Don't you guys think that's terrific?" Give him some credit! she wanted to add.

"How much you getting for that job?" Hub called out, a master of subtlety.

Paul grimaced, in a purely reflexive action. But today, for once, he was well armed. He tilted his head back, his voice mellifluous and carefree and airy. "Almost twenty-five thousand, Dad!" But Bronwyn could sense little cracks forming around the edges of the burnished smoothness. Just letting Hub get his big callused hands around figures could be dangerous, even if the figures were impressive, big ones.

"Ohhhh—*that's* quite a lot," Dorothy murmured, but still frowning. Bronwyn squeezed Paul's hand, gave him the thumbs-up signal. It *was* a lot. So it was more like $17,500 after taxes. So it was spread out over ten months. The point was, this wasn't for teaching, or typing, or even painting apartments, it was for *writing*. Paul was being paid to write!

"Hmph. The real question is . . ." Hub's large white-haired forearms muscled the wheel to the right. "How many times a year do you get paid twenty-five thousand?"

"Dad." Dorothy shushed Hub disapprovingly. That was Dorothy's role. While Dorothy might carry the same hysterical doubts about Paul's and Bronwyn's lives in L.A. as Hub, her job was to mete out the worried parental questioning in tiny bite-size chunks so the children would not just be swept away in a Florida-size hurricane.

Bronwyn bit her lip. Well, if abuse was to be taken, it should at least be spread equally. Bronwyn raised her voice again, letting little bells ring through it. "If you want to hear about big business breakthroughs, the person you should be talking to is Jonathan! *He's* been doing awfully well lately!"

"Yeah—did you hear about Jonathan?" Paul broke in with new enthusiasm. "Good one!" he mouthed. They exchanged silent snickers.

"What did you do, dear?" Dorothy painfully twisted her shoulders so she could gaze upon her eldest with polite interest.

"Sold some computer software," Jonathan called out, scowling, from his hunched position in the back. He was squashed into the child's jump seat, his knees up to his ears. He looked understandably reluctant to have information pried from him.

"Well, good for you, son!" Hub erupted. "The Golden Boy!" A billboard proclaiming "Chicken Palace" flashed by on their left. Hub pounded the steering wheel, enthusiastic. "It's this new computer wave, Dorothy—by George, he knows these computers!"

"Brilliant we always knew he was," Dorothy agreed, allowing a small smile to flit across her habitually bereft countenance. "That's our Jonathan. Oh, Paul has always been the imaginative one, no doubt about that." It obviously pained her to say the word "imaginative," carrying, as it did, all of its "lost at sea" implications. "But when it comes to brains—"

"And marketing, marketing!" Hub narrowed his eyes on the road, held up his fist as though trying to grab some elusive quality out of the air. "Jonathan has always had that . . . what's the word? That business *savvy*! You could learn a thing or two from him, Paul," he added, leaning back, giving a sober nod of the head.

The Flamingo's Rest trailer park looked much like the ones Bronwyn had seen in movies. ("Because even the flamingos sometimes have to lie down a spell," was how Paul had explained the name. "After all that bingo, they're just exhausted.") Under the setting Florida sun, row after row of senior-citizen mobile homes were arranged along almost comically neat asphalt streets and tiny patches of hopeful lawn.

To Bronwyn's eyes, it all seemed uniquely *real*.

In L.A., she reflected, you had people continually posing as things other than themselves. Wearing hats that were knockoffs of unaffordable stuff from the "Style" pages of *LA LA* magazine. Pouring jug wine into fluted glasses. Pretending to have read people like Foucault, or to know what John Cale and Brian Eno did on their last albums.

Here people were no one but themselves. They had no shame about it. They had no inkling that they should ever behave otherwise. And the effect, as one walked up and down the rows, was

amazing—visually arresting—beyond any Red Grooms instal-
lation.

Here were the lawn elves, the bumper stickers—"God Bless
Our Trailer" and "If the Trailer's A-Rockin', Don't Come A-
Knockin'!" Hunched Winnebago and Tioga cabs with eerily festive awnings squatted behind wooden signs—"The Solvings!" or
"The Johanssens!" majestic as though trumpeting the Hearst cas-
tle. "Merle and Lois Ostergaard Welcome You!" roared another
one, carved out of pieces of driftwood.

"Driftwood," Bronwyn marveled to Paul. "When did you last
see *that*? And do you realize that this sign implies there's a human
being on this planet whose name is actually Merle Ostergaard?"

"Merle Ostergaard!" Paul exclaimed. "I think I've met him. He
used to play the accordion at VFW dances in Sioux Falls!"

"Merle Ostergaard plays the accordion at VFW dances," Bronwyn repeated, stunned by the sentence's sheer linguistic invention.

"And can you believe *this*?" Bronwyn murmured, once they
returned to the elder Hoffsteads' gently swaying mobile home (the
"mother ship," Paul called it).

On a corkboard wall in the tiny kitchen, underneath the
wooden "Busy Bee Good Neighbor Club" placard, was pinned,
importantly, in a place of honor—right opposite the tiny breakfast
nook, right in optimum guest eyeshot—Jonathan's blue and white
printed business card. "Hoffstead Software Systems," it declared,
and then, without a shred of shame: "President." Also proudly
displayed was a sheet of stationery from Hoffstead Software
Systems.

But their eye-opening field trip to America's heartland was just
beginning.

"We're taking you kids all out to dinner!" Hub bellowed, as he shrugged on his natty rust-colored circa 1967 corduroy jacket with leather epaulets and elbow pads. Dorothy was shrugging into a sensible baby-blue windbreaker that had fake fur around the hood. Her white tennis shoes stuck sensibly out below her white and powder-blue houndstooth slacks.

This was bad news. When Hub treated, it was never elegant.

"Dad, I insist," Paul protested. "I thought we decided in the car that *we* would take *you* out—"

"It's *your* golden wedding anniversary!" Bronwyn cried out, desperate.

"I won't hear of it!" Hub retorted, holding up his hand, apparently delighted to be sliding back, at this late juncture of life, into his patriarch's chair. "You kids all flew yourselves out here—at great expense I know—"

Actually, Dorothy had secretly mailed a check for Paul's, Jonathan's, and Bronwyn's tickets. That had been before Paul's new job, though. He swore he'd pay them back.

"And you've all taken time off work," Dorothy hurriedly interceded, to keep the level of factuality as high as reasonably possible. "Which we know costs money," she added forgivingly, patting Bronwyn's hand.

"It's just that we know tomorrow's party must have put you back quite a bit," Bronwyn persisted. "And we'd like to do a little something for you after all you've done for us. We are making really good money now, finally, and the least we can do—"

"And besides, you're—you're retired," Paul bumbled forward. "It's not like your Social Security income could be all that much! You really need to start thinking about your *own*—"

"Oh, Hub isn't doing all that poorly." Dorothy nodded curtly, in her birdlike fashion. She didn't seem to take much delight in this news; then again, it didn't seem to displease her. "He had a few things roll over." On the words "roll over," her plump white hand gave a sudden curving little flip, like a dolphin hopping over a wave. "And he finally let the old Pine Cove cabin go for quite a tidy sum, quite a tidy sum."

"Pine Cove?" Paul erupted, stung. "I didn't know you guys still had that!"

"Oh yes," Dorothy replied, in her unflappable, precise fashion. "Your father thought he'd hold on to it a bit longer. Turned out to be the right thing to do, let me tell you."

The restaurant choice of the lucky investor was a family-style place called Chin's Chinese Kitchen. Apparently a chain restaurant, it featured an all-you-can-eat Chinese buffet ($6.99 a dinner) flanked by red paper scrolls with plastic white Buddhas everywhere. Kenny G music floated overhead.

"An all-you-can-eat Chinese buffet?" Bronwyn whispered to Paul. They stood with their pink plastic trays before a gleaming center island which contained pans of slippery chow mein and vegetables and beef chunks all sliding together. Under a heat lamp stood trays of deep-fried egg rolls. And a pan of fries. At the far end were tureens of what appeared to be chicken noodle soup. Beyond that, that most Oriental of culinary inventions—a salad bar.

The place was packed—absolutely packed—with white-haired Floridians. Ka-ching, ka-ching! went the cash register.

When they got to the proverbial end of the line, Bronwyn threw caution to the winds and ordered a big glass of Chablis.

"After all, your dad just had a few things roll over," she hissed to Paul, mimicking Dorothy's dolphin hand motion. "I'm sure he can stretch his resources just a little farther."

It was when they'd all set their cafeteria trays down together that Hub finally let them have it.

"So when are you kids going to move away from that hellhole L.A.?"

"I beg your pardon?" Bronwyn asked, her deep-fried egg roll halting midway to her mouth.

"Now, now, Hub," Dorothy murmured, as though trying to shush a wayward child.

"What do you got there?" Hub humorously ticked off the points on his large white hand. "Smog, crime, earthquakes . . . I don't get it! In South Dakota, we've got clean air, clean water, good schools, new hospitals. It's nice that you get one film job, Paul—but that's one job in . . . what is it? Six years? Are you two building up a savings account even? Where are—"

"Come, now." Dorothy patted Hub's hand. "I'm sure California has many nice features as well." Her face settled into its mask of worry as she twirled her chow mein around her fork, as though it were spaghetti.

"Like what?" Hub wondered with faux naïveté, wide-eyed.

"Like Hollywood," Dorothy put in, the barest hint of balefulness infecting her voice. "Pauly *has* to live in L.A. It's the only place he can do his films, the only place."

"But have you ever thought of it?" Hub put his chopsticks down and leaned forward, the excitement of his hardy German ancestors lighting up his blue eyes. "Moving back to Sioux Falls? Moving to Texas maybe to be near cousin Eileen? *She's* got an awfully good thing going with those banks and things, relocating—what is it?—California aircraft companies to other states with friendlier business regulations . . ."

"Why don't you ask Jonathan these questions?" Paul flashed out, his controlled, burnished vocal tones a distant memory. "What—am I the only casualty of Los Angeles?"

Jonathan merely rolled his eyes, let his mouth go slack, and continued eating.

"Jonathan can run his computer company from anywhere," Dorothy explained patiently, putting her arm around Jonathan. "And he's still a bachelor, for gosh sakes. He's always traveled light. Jonathan will always land on his feet. He has a knack for it. But you and Bronwyn—well, you'll be wanting to start a family soon—"

"You need to start building some kind of life!" Hub pleaded, opening his huge palms. "My God—"

"Hub!" Dorothy corrected him sharply.

"Excuse me. It's just that you're both thirty. I don't see what kind of future you're building out there in L.A.!"

"What he means is, when are you going to get married?" Dorothy murmured. "You've been living together for—what, seven years?"

"Our plan has always been to get married when Paul sells his first big . . . script," Bronwyn said staunchly, squeezing Paul's hand under the table. He squeezed it back, hard.

"Isn't this thing a script?" Hub asked.

"But it's . . . an industrial," Paul explained. "It's not the big one."

"The big one," Hub repeated, grimly amused by the concept.

"Well, there's one way in which Southern California is far, far ahead of anyplace else in the U.S.," Bronwyn heard herself remark, before she could stop herself.

All heads turned toward her.

"What?"

What had caused her to butt in? She never did, with Paul's parents.

"Um, real estate," she said. "Or at least that's—you know, what I've been hearing."

"Real estate," Dorothy repeated.

There was a pause.

Beyond Hub and Dorothy's twin white heads, and even the somewhat disheveled brown heads of Paul and Jonathan, Bronwyn found herself oddly mesmerized by the vagaries of Chin's Chinese Kitchen, Buffet Dinner: $6.99. The bobbing cardigans of the trailer park seniors, the cheesy tasseled lanterns, the shiny salad bar, the brown mounds of chow mein under their heat lamps. At the far end of the restaurant was a portrait of Chin, a ghoulishly cheerful old Fu Manchu type brandishing a cleaver.

Chin's Chinese Kitchen was the very picture of Middle American kitsch.

But looking at it, Bronwyn felt only freedom, an odd elation.

Who cared what kind of kitchen it was? A Chinese kitchen. A Japanese kitchen. A Peruvian kitchen. These were all beautiful things.

Even the memory of Colin Martin's kitchen heartened her now. The copper pans, the white and blue tile, the garden window—it all symbolized the heady physical evidence of what was possible, what could be home.

Bronwyn put her chopsticks down, deliberately chewing

through the last of her beef, and felt the glory of her vision increase. She found all the words and facts channeling back to her—stringing together Colin Martin statements with quotes from the Zibby Tanaka manual she had read on the plane with—who knows where else she had heard this? On NPR? At UCLA?

It didn't matter: it was all coming together.

"In the last few years," she instructed the group, "property has been appreciating there like you wouldn't believe. It's a boom time for real estate in Los Angeles."

Dorothy's chopsticks froze in the air. "Yes. I think . . . I have . . . heard . . . of that." Her chopsticks tapped precisely with each word.

Bronwyn leaned forward into the light. "It's that constant influx." The moment she said the magic word that Colin had used, the conviction descended upon her. In her mind's eye, she saw Diversity 2000 families—professionals, in tortoiseshell rims and tailored suits—in Volvo station wagons, streaming along L.A.'s freeways toward the center of the city, the hub. They had laptop computers, and claw-foot bathtubs, and terra-cotta vases, and sushi makers, and—and these menorah things and nowhere to lay them down.

The vision was almost epic.

"Los Angeles is becoming a new world center. People are streaming in from major capitals all over the Pacific Rim—"

"The Pacific Rim?" Dorothy inquired politely.

"Asia, South America, North America. Immigrants are coming in from all over, creating a dynamic mixture of cultures and ideas. Multiculturalism is what's making L.A. a new world center. The demand for housing is swelling. Our old schoolmate Colin Martin made a hundred and thirty thousand dollars out of a five-year investment."

"A hundred and thirty thousand? In five years?" Hub blew out air. "With Pine Cove, it took me nine years to make that much!"

"Actually, you cleared sixty thousand," Dorothy corrected him.

"That's right. If you count the tractor."

"And Colin made that on just a condo!"

"A condo?" Hub was amazed.

"You mean a condominium—an apartment?" Dorothy quizzed.

"Two bedrooms, one bath," Bronwyn pronounced. "A thousand square feet. It's out of control. Totally out of control."

And then she did something sly. Amid all her euphoria, she had a sly moment. "Just ask Jonathan," she threw out casually. "He's been thinking about buying property himself."

"You were?" Hub and Dorothy turned their attention excitedly to their most brilliant son.

It was that night that the dream burst into flower.

"Kids," Hub announced regally, as the family squished around the tiny breakfast nook table under the swaying lamp. He riffled through a kitchen drawer, lifted out what appeared to be dog-eared bank statements neatly rubber-banded together, those wrapped in turn in clear plastic bags. "As you know, your mother and I have been saving our pennies over the years . . ."

Bronwyn and Paul looked at each other questioningly.

Hub picked up Jonathan's hand, then Paul's hand. He put them down and picked up the rubber-banded bundles, hefted them as if they were gold bricks. "Today these mutual funds are worth about fifty-two thousand dollars."

"Fifty-two thousand!" Paul exclaimed.

Hub looked at Dorothy, who stood to one side, birdlike, vigilant. She nodded at him, lips pursed.

"It'll have to do for now," she said. "It'll have to do."

It was a thing the South Dakotan farm people always said. Like, "After even the coldest winter has to come the spring."

"We've been thinking about how difficult things have been for you in Los Angeles," Hub continued. "Things have been going good for us, and so now we want to loan you this money to help you now, help you . . . buy a piece of property. You with your imagination, Paul, Jonathan with his smarts, and even Bronwyn—" Hub picked up Bronwyn's hand, squeezed it. "Even Bronwyn with her business savvy! I'm sure you'll triple this money overnight!

"Then we can *really* retire in style!" Hub concluded, looking over his gently swaying mobile domain, winking at Dorothy.

Twenty-six thousand dollars. Lying awake later, on the foam pad she and Paul shared in the Winnebago, Bronwyn shivered, in awe. Twenty-six thousand . . . in one chunk? It was more money than she could imagine.

Between Paul's writing job and this . . . It was like a door to their future was swinging open, and instead of a turgid blasted landscape unfolding beyond, there was, unexpectedly, at the eleventh hour, a gorgeous valley bathed in dreamy sunlight. She could actually feel her shoulders unhunch, her back straighten, her brow relax, unwrinkle.

God, she wanted this money. She wanted. This money. Twenty-six thousand dollars. It was not a life raft but an ocean liner. She and Paul had been drowning in L.A. without even knowing it. With every bounced $26 check, every $5 of gas put into the car because she wasn't sure if $10 would clear the ATM, she had been gasping for breath. She had thought it was the smog that made the walls of their Tujunga house increasingly sooty over the years, but in fact it was the light around her, literally dimming.

Twenty-six thousand . . . They could spend $500 on new underwear and socks (when did they last buy those?) and—sushi . . . That's right. They could go eat sushi and not even have to drink all that water so they'd feel full after the third piece. They could eat $40 worth and not think twice. Five hundred dollars could be mad money.

They could sock a few thousand away in savings. Savings, she loved that word. It sounded so adult. She and Paul had never had savings. They had tried, one year, to put $50 away at a time. Their amassed sum—a paltry $450—had crumbled all in one fell swoop when the VW's carburetor went out. Health insurance had been their other impossible dream. Maybe they could start some of that up too.

That would leave $20,000—a huge sum—for a down payment on a house. At twenty percent . . . she quickly calculated. That would mean a $100,000 house. God. Incredible. Her parents' old house in San Jose had cost them—what? Forty-seven thousand? Of course that was many years ago. Real estate had gone up a lot. Especially in Los Angeles.

But still: $100,000. That would not land them in Beverly Hills, but certainly in a nice little suburb somewhere. There would be three bedrooms at least. A lovely yard, with huge oak trees.

Sprawling wooden deck. A rolling green lawn with room, way on down the line, for a swing set. When the children came, years later, after she and Paul had time to enjoy the place.

Probably, at $100,000, you'd get totally redone kitchens and bathrooms, one skylight somewhere, maybe even a brick fireplace. God. A brick fireplace. She loved that idea. How funny and suburban—almost like a throwback to their parents' time.

But who knew what they'd see, in the unpredictable sprawl of L.A. No doubt there would be some secret nook, some idyllic little cul-de-sac, waiting to surprise them. For now, she'd have to keep her eyes open and her imagination wide . . .

And this was the feeling—a feeling of wonder—that Bronwyn took with her to the Flamingo's Rest church choir the next morning. The "church" was held in the trailer park's assembly hall, the long Formica tables pushed to one side, orange plastic chairs set up in long exact rows facing a little stage, gold velour curtains, American flags drooping on either side. A plump senior in blue flower-print dress pounded a rickety yellow upright piano stage left.

To the new Bronwyn, reborn into the world of hope, this vision of Americana was the most wonderful thing she'd ever seen.

As she held her songbook, she looked out at the hundred or so gathered seniors of the Flamingo's Rest trailer park. She saw a sea of iron-gray and white heads, of weather-beaten, wrinkled faces, of sensible dark jackets, plaid shirts, flowered blouses.

Who were these seventy-something people, she thought, who saved their pennies in "rollover" accounts and drove thousands of miles every year to southern Florida?

Who were these people who rose Sunday morning at seven A.M.— from their rickety trailers—just to come to church?

Who were the people who now dutifully turned their song-books to page 47 to sing "More Love to You, Jesus, More Love to You"?

The Solvings. The Johanssens. The Ostergaards . . .

She nodded her head sagely, thinking of the trailer park streets. Cartoonish, yes, but secretly filled with blocks of power—blocks of power in rubber bands. And above it all, "immigrants" was the word that rose, mushrooming like a cloud.

Immigrants! Sure, now these seniors lived in the Midwest, where they were retired insurance adjusters, car salesmen, hardware store owners. But their ancestors were Norwegians, Germans, Dutch. They'd been potato farmers—grim, gray-haired folk, straight as ramrods, who'd coaxed a tough living from hard rocky land year after year after year in cold, cold lands.

For their descendants, then, getting up at seven A.M. was easy—particularly when all you had to do was sit on your duff, praise the Lord, and sing. Compared to their ancestors, they *were* living the good life now, in their lawn chairs, in their mobile homes, playing bingo, free as old wrinkled birds . . .

And for *their* descendants, even a better life would unfold. Because these hardy folk were all just another part of the great chain of immigration, the same one pushing L.A.'s property values through the roof. The same one that had given Paul his job . . .

Even the beleaguered Colonial American women poets were part of this immigrant chain, Bronwyn noted sagely. She felt it coming full circle. Hammering tables, making pickles—they'd been immigrants too. And perhaps scholars should leave them alone. Those Colonial American women had enough troubles without us poking and prodding at them, she thought, expecting them to do *so* much more than they originally set out to.

Maybe Jane Ann Williams just *wanted* to write letters! Maybe that was enough! Maybe she'd quail to think we were sifting through them today, analyzing metaphors, arguing significance!

"Let me be!" she imagined Jane Ann Williams exclaiming to a fustering Shirley Kent. Knowing Jane, she'd probably be jabbing at Dr. Kent with a whisk broom. "Just let me be!" Bronwyn knew exactly how Jane Ann Williams felt. Sometimes you just wanted to be allowed to continue to be . . . mediocre. Perhaps all you wanted to do was redecorate your kitchen. Festoon it with sweet-smelling . . . potpourri. Shine your pots.

How ironic that it was only now she finally understood the Colonial American women poets—now that she was no longer going to be studying them!

Finally, Bronwyn saw that she and Paul were immigrants too. What stranger land could there be than Los Angeles? What odder customs and people could Paul and she ever have imagined? How much less prepared could they be to assimilate themselves?

But Bronwyn, pioneering woman, would help her man, as so many other women had helped theirs before her.

Oh, she felt that she had never been so incredibly connected to—to the very idea of women and their often quiet, unspectacular struggles.

She even understood Dorothy now.

Many people from L.A., she thought, would have considered Hub and Dorothy's golden anniversary festivities tacky. They occurred during the unfashionable hours between one and three P.M. in the unfashionable mess hall—its Formica tables and orange plastic chairs reconfigured back to their usual position. Refreshments consisted of a light snack of coconut cake, mixed Planters nuts, and nonalcoholic Hawaiian Punch. Seated on the tiny stage was the sixty-something band—"Don Turlock and His Texas Teddies."

But for the first time, as the band played, Bronwyn got a glimpse of the winsome young girl Dorothy had once been. In her stocking feet, Paul's mother, dimpling and blushing, rolled into a surprisingly energetic swing step. Meanwhile, Don Turlock and His Texas Teddies sang:

"Skirts! I love those skirts!"

On the word "skirts," Dorothy's plump white hands flew out together in a skimming motion. "Skirts!" she mouthed, and twirled, her portly figure showing an amazing fluidity. "I love those skirts!"

"Well, congratulations, Dorothy," Bronwyn murmured. "Fifty years of marriage! What could be harder to pull off than *that*?" She looked across the room and saw Paul, talking to Hub and smiling for a brief unworried moment.

She had the image of Paul as a slender but resilient reed, who bent in storm after storm after storm but did not break. She thought of herself and Paul lasting fifty years and a tear came to her eye.

Hub and Dorothy had lasted fifty years. Fifty years. Who knew what these folks had suffered? They probably had struggled, just like she and Paul had, but they had made it. Because . . .

"After even the coldest winter has to come the spring."

Of course.

She raised her glass of nonalcoholic punch to the Flamingo's Rest seniors, twirling across the dance floor, the endless ribbon of generations, surprisingly debonair with their clipped gray hair and suit jackets and floral-print dresses.

part two

———

high-rise

tachometer readings

Downtown!

Before this evening, Bronwyn had never realized how stunning it was . . . how you careened around the 5 and hit the top of Dodger Stadium hill and all at once the ground fell away before you and there it was . . .

Downtown, its glass towers, shards, discs, and spears rising eerily from the L.A. basin. A bejeweled starship, its gravitational beam tracked you in, pulling you into its maw, its glass elevators beetling, its phone lines humming—L.A.'s mysterious hub, its nucleus, its core.

Of course, never before had she approached downtown at sixty-five miles per hour, winging along in a *brand-new car!*

Their new car. Their sporty, electric-blue, 1991 Geo Futura, black interior, spoiler, mag wheels, moonroof. The nubbed grip of the wheel, the confident glow of speedometer, tachometer, RPMs, and who knew what else, the shine of the curved windshield, the smooth sleekness of its black dashboard, the cab climate shifting—with the faintest exhale—at the touch of a button.

And what a perfect world surrounded this perfect car . . .

Before her, a line of red taillights, like beads on a necklace, streamed toward the sparkling center of the city.

Above her, the deep blue night. Okay, the deep-blue-leaning-toward-brown night—making a kind of L.A. maroon. Whatever. The point was, the moonroof made the sky seem as though it were hers, all hers.

Behind her: Tujunga . . . and the shuddering VW bus.

Bronwyn felt a pang.

It had happened last week: the VW bus's clutch had gone out for the last time.

Bronwyn and Paul had been prepared, as usual, to hunker down, wincing, and write out another check for not a new clutch ($700) but a sort of a . . . "rebuilt" one ($400).

But then the snub-nosed mechanic began his litany.

Rebuilding the VW clutch would not work anymore. It had been rebuilt so many times there was no original piece of clutch on it. They'd have to go for a whole new one—the price of which had gone up to $900. Also, they really should put in an extra $250 for the left front axle boot. "The brakes are down around twenty percent too," he had added, shaking his head. "Makes it really kind of dangerous to drive in. Cost you—ahhhh, another two or so."

Come to think of it, what about the passenger's-side window, the one that didn't roll down all the way? And how about the heater? The one that hadn't worked since Jimmy Carter's presidency. Shouldn't that be fixed too? And hey, look at those rear tires. Pretty darn bald, the right one with that slow leak you had to attend to twice a week. New seats too might be nice, ones that didn't have lumps in them, whose coils didn't squeak when you shifted, and perhaps a new leather cover for the steering wheel with its uncoiling plastic . . .

"But the VW bus is so much more than that," Bronwyn had protested to Paul. "It's more than just the sum of its parts—"

What she wanted to say was: "Don't you remember why we got it? To connect with history! Berkeley in the sixties! Ken Kesey! Abbie Hoffman! Woodstock!"

What she said instead was: "We were going to have adventures in it! Take that trip around the Pacific Northwest. See the . . . Redwoods."

"Noni," Paul said softly, taking her hand. "We've never had any great adventures in the VW bus and never will. It's always breaking down. Besides . . ." His brows knit together. "I have a real job now. I need something dependable to get to work in."

The VW mechanic had directed them to the pleasant people at Skip Miller Chevy/Geo in Glendale. After listening, soberly, to their plight, the salespeople proposed that Bronwyn and Paul unload the VW for $1,000. This could then go toward a down payment on their choice of a brand-new '91 Hyundai Scoupe or '91 Geo Futura, which could be literally driven off the lot for just $1,800 down and forty-eight months of easy $218 monthly payments. Ten-thousand-mile warranty included.

Bronwyn had to admit that it did sound reasonable.

And so, the two mechanics in orange jumpsuits hustled the battered white VW bus away. The battered white VW bus, with its lovingly preset public broadcasting radio buttons—KCRW, KPFK, KPCC, KUSC, KLON—its fading "Women's Studies" bumper sticker, the license plate frame that said "Save the Forests" . . .

And the purple batik scarf that Bronwyn had forgotten to untie from around the rearview mirror!

The purple batik scarf!

Bronwyn threw out an arm after it, let out a cry.

"Let it go, Noni," Paul said again, holding her back. "Let it go."

And now Bronwyn began to feel the guilt.

Just what were they planning to do to the old VW in the vast, canyonlike back lot of Skip Miller Chevy/Geo? Break it into salvage? Bash at it with two-by-fours? Drive it over the Palisades and film it plunging ignominiously into the Pacific—Herbie's real Last Stand?

With a resigned sigh, Bronwyn slipped the smooth, black, futuristically rounded key into the ignition of the Futura.

She turned it. Nothing happened.

But the dashboard lights, everything was on.

Bronwyn hadn't realized it, but after driving the VW bus for so many years she had come to associate "on" with the whole cab swaying from side to side while rattling really, really loudly and coughing.

"Is it possible for a car really to be this quiet?"

She and Paul looked at each other in surprise, then broke out into amazed laughter.

All right: so what if this brand-new Geo had no history— sixties, Woodstock, or otherwise. It had a future ... in fact, a whole new *Futura*. And maybe so could they.

Driving the Futura, Bronwyn found that she felt easy and light and—and oddly sporty, yes sporty ... a brand new person with a moonroof and a spoiler and mag wheels who would think nothing of whizzing along a beach in the sunset, if she so wished, gaily clinking a wineglass with her date, a jazz saxophonist serenading them—leaning back in ecstasy, sun glinting off his horn—from atop a craggy, wave-battered rock . . .

The beach. They could go to the beach in this thing. Sure. Why not?

For years, of course, Bronwyn and Paul, black-clad Bohemians, had sworn that if they did move to L.A. they would never set foot on the beach. It would be much too Southern California cliché, the sun itself symbolic of a creeping evil of blandness surrounding them on every side . . .

"We're not sun people," Paul would say.

"That's right," she'd reply.

"We're not pro-sun. We're anti-sun."

But where exactly had all these rules come from? And why did she and Paul obey them so stringently?

". . . in Somalia," NPR murmured. "Forty-seven dead. Meanwhile, in Simi Valley, California, reports continue from the courthouse that—"

"My God!" Bronwyn cried out, back in real time, something snapping inside her. "Is it never enough? Is it never enough?"

Somalia, Serbia, Simi Valley, all the shootings, stabbings, murders—was there any trouble in the world that NPR would not cover? It seemed as though no matter what temporary fleeting joy Bronwyn might feel in this life, there NPR would always stand, muttering in her ear, plucking her elbow with worry:

"Hey Bronwyn, enough about you. Do you realize that at this very second children are starving in a city with corrupt policemen on the dole who are robbing postal trucks and bombings continue in the terrorist left bank of the capital of the Communist centrist barracks of the city that has no water because of the Dow chemical spill in the . . ."

With one bold gesture, swift as an executioner, Bronwyn reached forward and did it.

She turned off NPR.

Silence thrummed through the electric blue Geo Futura, with its glowing speedometer, tachometer . . .

"Oh my God," she whispered. "Oh my God.

But the ceiling—the moonroof, actually—did not fall in. Her world didn't crazily turn upside down, the Geo capsizing into a dark gulch. She didn't feel a clutch at her throat, of some fatal disease of the soul coming on. Through polished glass, the gleaming spires of downtown L.A.—a vision, she thought now, a veritable vision of the future—still approached. In the distance, in fact, she saw a welcoming banner hanging across one of the towers. The letters read: "IF YOU LIVED HERE, YOU'D BE HOME BY NOW!"

Bronwyn saw all this and felt . . .

Silence. Calm. Peace.

"Oh my God," she repeated.

And then, the hand that moments ago she'd thought she controlled did not withdraw. Rather, it flicked over to the polished black tuning button, touching it until the blue digital numbers of the dial read . . . 94.7. The Wave.

The Wave. It was the worst thing. The Wave radio station— "smooth jazz," "adult contemporary music"—was the very symbol of the encroaching, numbing evil of the eighties.

"New Age pap!" she and Paul used to cry out together, after they had heard it on in someone else's house. "Yuppie elevator music! Escapist drivel! How can they put that on?"

Her finger moved again. Volume up. Some sort of winsome flute was undulating over a breathy, slightly funky background—

"I'm doing it," she whispered, "I am actually listening to the Wave!"

It was totally brainless, yes. "Nah na na na dwa-a-a da!" a laughing Brazilian woman confided. "Dat da da da dwa-a-a da!" The music brought to mind a cool, shaded café overlooking some lush tropical island in the Caribbean. It was all vaguely Club Med, all sandy and blue with hammocks.

Experimentally, Bronwyn pressed the button to tilt her plush bucket seat back, dropped her shoulders back.

Who am I? she thought. Who am I?

"Dat da da da dwa-a-a da!" the laughing Brazilian woman continued, seeming to nudge Bronwyn. The Brazilians. The eternally permissive Brazilians, those bronze-toned enablers. "Oh come on," Bronwyn imagined the woman saying, "take off your shoes. Samba with us—samba with us in the sand! We are so happy, here on this island. Have an umbrella drink!"

"All ri-i-ight!" the DJ said reverently. "That was 'Island Samba' by Gloria Johnston and the Latin jazz group Wind . . . Jammer. Remember too that tickets are still available for next week's Global Music Festival at the Greek, featuring Steve Halpert and his Juju Music Band, Henry Rice and Gondwalaland Morning, Zydeco Sunset featuring—"

Listening to the Wave—this yuppie drivel—meant you were one of Them, the faceless yuppie masses.

At the same time, making a big point of not listening to the Wave just meant you were one of the Others—the faceless *non*-yuppie masses . . .

The dyed-in-the-wool Bohemians.

The people of Trader Joe's.

Trader Joe's.

Bronwyn drew her breath in, shook her head.

Many years ago, when they had first moved to Tujunga, Bronwyn had discovered, in nearby La Crescenta, a wonderful quaint little store called Trader Joe's. It was classical music, Swedish chocolates, frozen Indian tikka masala dinners, exotically named Chardonnays . . . all at bargain prices that she could afford. She thought it was just a cute little La Crescenta thing, her own personal stroke of good fortune, something that gave her a leg up on this city.

And so, she loved to give parties for their friends, to share her good fortune with them.

For the food table, she'd always buy this wonderful sort of rugged pâté, salmon spread, Brie, French bread. She liked to arrange it all on a cutting board, with perhaps a sprig of grapes from Lucky's to one side. She had a nice basket for them, one she'd purchased on sale one day ($4.99) at, of course, the Four Winds Emporium.

She'd pick up a few bottles of Trader Joe's Burgundy and Chardonnay and put them out on the same table. Not the big jugs but actual regular-size bottles! True, most were $1.99 each—she was careful to peel off the labels. But still, there was a sense that a person could contemplate a few different bottles, consider their merits, and select one. They might be in Northern California, they might be in Berkeley.

"Mm . . . Brie!" people usually said. "I love Brie!"

Of course they did. Soft French cheese was a delightful surprise, Bronwyn had thought at the time, in the cultural desert that was Southern California . . .

The following week, Paul and Bronwyn were invited to a party given by Sandy, a USC film graduate student Paul had met at AFI.

Sandy had a cute two-bedroom in the Fairfax district which boasted a lot of beautiful tile in the kitchen and bathroom. Not much else—there was a water pressure problem and Sandy's roommate had been mugged in front of their place the night before. So Bronwyn felt a little bit ahead of them in that.

But then Bronwyn came to the food table. There, on a burgundy-color paper tablecloth, was the familiar cutting board. To one side were the grapes—in that same Four Winds Emporium basket! My God! They had gone to the same sale!

Her heart in her mouth, Bronwyn crept forward, the noise of the unshaven graduate students, the hanging Japanese paper lanterns from the Four Winds Emporium around her like a blur. All she saw was that table. She came closer.

And there it was. The wedge of rubbery Brie. The dark pâté. The salmon spread. And . . .

Bronwyn felt as though she had been hit by a bus.

The brave little bottles of $1.99 Trader Joe's wine.

Did everybody, everybody, absolutely everybody, have a Trader Joe's at their corner?

Apparently yes. Over the weeks that followed, as in a Kafka nightmare, Bronwyn started to see—everywhere, absolutely everywhere—the red signs of the Trader Joe's . . . on National Boulevard in West L.A., California Boulevard in Pasadena, Sherman Oaks! In lockstep, all of the self-described Bohemians were pulling out Brie and pâté with grubby hands, hurling them on cutting boards, draping them sloppily with the day-old Lucky's grapes.

Team Bohemia was as conventional and nonindividual and—and faceless as those hideous college sports teams who wore letter sweaters and special rings—

And so, dammit, if Bronwyn wanted to listen to the Wave, she would! Because she could! She was not afraid of anyone's censure! She sort of liked this Brazilian music, dammit!

Bronwyn continued to determinedly hum the "Island Samba" tune—"Dat da da da dwa-a-a da!"—as she pulled off the Temple Street exit, parked the Futura in the too-expensive but really quite convenient $7 parking garage, melded in with the other glamorously dressed people mounting the stairs to the Music Center Plaza.

"Dat da da da dwa-a-a da! Dat da da da dwa-a-a da!"

And when she reached the top, the sky opened above her and all was beauty.

The Music Center Plaza!

The spotlights. The coursing fountains. The couples in glimmering evening dresses and handsome suit jackets roamed the terrace, greeting and nodding to each other. Lights winked in the trees. Colorful banners flapped above.

"Dat da da da dwa-a-a da!" she hummed again, quickening her step.

And then ahead of her, a tall, broad-shouldered man—lightly tousled blond hair, manly jaw, a clean powerful figure in a black tux—split from the silhouetted throng of concertgoers and hurried down marble stairs toward her. Almost like in a Chanel ad.

"Bronwyn!" he called out. "How beautiful you look!"

"Colin!" she called back, her heart, for a moment, caught in her throat with the splendor of him.

save the children

Harold King—two-time Oscar winner, five-time Emmy winner, with three gold and one platinum record-production credits to his name, a dear friend and colleague of "Theme to St. Elmo's Fire" composer David Foster and of Carol Bayer Sager and, on top of all that, brand new chairperson of the Children of El Salvador Foundation—stood in the hard white spotlight, his manicured hands clasped before him, his shaggy gray mane bowed.

He wanted to move forward with the program, but couldn't.

The tuxedoed and gowned crowd gathered under the plush chandeliered dome of the Dorothy Chandler Pavilion—earrings and cuff links glinting here and there, a sudden skinny exposed back beyond, the slitted flash of a perfect young leg—appeared to want to just clap on and on.

After a minute or so, Harold King's shaggy head lifted slightly. One white hand in neat Armani cuff floated upward—

But this gesture of humility just made his glittering audience's cheering more wild.

He shook his head: in surrender, the head and hand dropped down again.

Finally, after what seemed like three minutes, he lifted his noble head and was allowed to speak.

"I am so honored," he murmured, his voice surprisingly caressing, mellifluous, "to be standing before such wonderful friends and colleagues this evening. And for such an urgent, important cause. I am standing here for one reason and one reason only. The children. The children who cannot help themselves, the children whose voices cry out in the night, the children who have never known anything but fear. The children of El Salvador."

The Children of El Salvador Music to Our Ears Charity Evening turned out to be a program of medley after medley of film music themes, conducted by Hollywood's biggest film music composers, performed by the BMI Foundation Young Adult Orchestra, seated stiffly on the stage in black concert dress.

First came the Coronation, Love, and Chase themes from Paramount's *King Arthur* scored by René Alexander, full of so much sudden orchestral swelling, such passionate reiteration of the same motifs over and over again modulating ever upward like the chorus of a Barry Manilow song, that Bronwyn felt bloated and even rather distended by the end of its twenty minutes.

Then came the "Clair de Lune"-ish—even up to the telltale ascending scales—overture from Warner Brothers' *Beluga,* last year's surprising blockbuster about a rapping inner-city kid who befriends and soon releases an Alaskan whale from captivity.

Not only had Bronwyn not heard of composer Larry Danielson, she had not heard of his—apparently recent—Movie of the Week, *Crash Landing: The Story of Flight 447.*

But for Larry Danielson, Bronwyn's—or anyone's else's—ignorance was of no concern. In a slightly ill-fitting tux, a ring of straggly gray hair crowning his bald pate, Danielson turned majestically to the BMI Foundation Young Adult Orchestra, as if he were about to give them *The Rite of Spring*.

He raised his baton . . . and with one vicious poke elicited an ominous timpani roll that was as loud as a shot.

The timpani roll roared over the tuxedoed audience who waited rapt in the darkness, and rolled, and rolled again.

Larry pumped, pumped, pumped the rhythm, letting the timpani ri-i-ise and fall, ri-i-ise and fall, ri-i-ise and fall.

Worriedly, the string section came in, its arpeggios hovering and rising and dipping like an airplane in stormy weather. Muted trumpets echoed in the distance. Rat a tat a tat! Rat a tat a tat! An electric piano suddenly contributed its nervous comments, via an almost seventies spy theme: Put a pling! Put a pling! Plingee! Plingee! Plong.

Then all at once, Larry Danielson became excited to the point of musical apoplexy. His entire torso seized forward, his tuxedo jacket rode up, sweat flew from his forhead. He threw his hands out as if he were plunging over a thousand-foot cliff.

At that exact second the timpani thundered out again and there was a deafening crash of cymbals. In came the tubas and double basses on a note so low Bronwyn felt her chest cavity vibrate: Bla-a-a-at! Bla-a-a-at! Bla-a-a-at! A piece of Movie of the Week disaster dialogue came to her mind: "Oh my God! We've lost hydraulics in engine number three!"

But the emotional high point of the evening came at its end. Two and a half hours in, Harold King himself returned to the stage, sitting at the gleaming ten-foot black Steinway. Surprised applause greeted pop singer Peabo Bryson, also resplendent in his tux.

Accompanied by Harold, Peabo Bryson began singing a simple Harold King ballad, penned for the occasion.

"Children . . . sa-a-ave the children?" he intoned somberly, almost as though in question.

A hush fell over the audience.

"Why can't you-ou-ou-ou see? The hope that there can be—"

As Peabo Bryson continued to softly sing, a slim forty-something woman with a perfect auburn pageboy in a cream-colored sheath walked radiantly out into the spotlight, leading by the hand a tiny dark-haired girl in matching lacy cream-colored dress. They wore identical white cloches. The little girl looked no more than two years old. She stumbled along on chubby legs, blinking in the light.

His hands still caressing the piano keyboard, Harold King stood. When his final chord had faded, he lifted a hand toward woman and girl, and announced: "Ladies and gentleman, my wife Petra . . .

"And may we introduce our newly adopted daughter, who arrived just forty-eight hours ago from El Salvador: Natalie Marie King."

With a gasp, the entire number who were gathered there rose from their seats and broke into tumultuous applause.

"So, how *are* you?" Bronwyn asked Colin, as he handed her a glass of champagne.

As she did so often in L.A., Bronwyn felt as though she were in a scene from some movie.

But for once, it was not an entirely unpleasant one.

Piano music murmured in the background; beyond them tuxedos and gowns moved in a stately arc. Beyond that ring of beautiful people, Harold and Petra King, the celebrities of the hour, held court. Above them all, like a cloud, wafted that trademark Hollywood conversation: "Vestron," "Lorimar" . . . which still sounded to Bronwyn like "Bla bla bla bla bla."

And also, for once, Bronwyn felt not like a faceless extra but a character with an identity, purpose, lines. Paul had shared some story ideas the other day that she thought, she could see, maybe, might be good for television. And here was their old friend Colin Martin—or hers, at least—a high-up muck-a-muck in television. And here Colin had invited her to this charity thing.

She hated television, but for Paul she would do anything.

She would talk to Colin about it. Or try to.

"How is life at . . . ABC?" she tried again, aiming for a tad more specificity.

"Oh, you don't really want to hear about that, do you?"

"Of course I do." She turned to him. "It's what you do. It's your work."

And so, with a show of reluctance, but picking up steam as he went along, Colin launched into his litany.

"It's just terribly depressing sometimes. It's all so formulaic. Occasionally something good does get through—if the bean-counters don't wreck it . . ."

"I had a meeting last week with Penny Marshall. Wonderful work. But of course the networks won't this, the networks won't that . . ."

"Television is *not* a medium that encourages ingenuity. If only there were some real writers working in Hollywood, maybe . . ."

"Uh-huh," Bronwyn said. "How interesting." She cautiously took a sip of champagne. Oh wow. The champagne whispered, delicate as antique lace. It was an entirely new experience in drinking. It made you feel reverent, want to drink it slowly, sip it—not throw it down like Gallo. She was trying to keep her focus on the bla bla bla, but found the room itself was beginning to envelop her like a delightful toasty fur.

Lex Ristorante. Who even knew such places existed, places where a dinner salad cost $8, a calamari appetizer $14? With its deep leather booths, antique red lamps, and Oriental carpets, there was a wonderful muted atmosphere to the place. The hush of money, Bronwyn thought. No single item immediately drew the eye, but once your gaze settled on one particular area, more and more subtle layers were revealed. Oh my God, you'd think, is that—thin gold trim on that embossed eggshell soup plate?

"But enough about me," Colin said. "I'm boring you with this depressing TV talk. How are you? I'm so sorry we didn't get much of a chance to chat last December. Hi, Frank," he noted in passing to, Bronwyn presumed, one of his fellow ABC-ers.

"Thanks for the donation to the Homeless Fund, Colin!" the man said. "Very generous."

"Don't mention it," said Colin. "We do what we can."

He turned back to her.

"You kind of—ran off. I felt like there was so much we still had to catch up on. I didn't even ask you about how your Ph.D. was going."

Bronwyn was really enjoying this champagne and noted that

even with what she thought were her tiny, reverent sips, she had drained half her glass whereas Colin's was still almost full.

"Colin," she said sincerely, "I am not doing the Ph.D. I quit."

Colin almost visibly recoiled. "But Bronwyn! For years, all you . . . all you talked about was going on in academia, writing, teaching, all the great issues—"

She shook her head violently.

She knew she should move on, press on with her mission, to ask Colin if he would look at Paul's stuff, but found that the champagne bubbles and the warmth and the giggling inside her were totally throwing her off her game . . .

At that moment, a waiter appeared beside her with more flutes of that marvelous champagne.

"Oh I couldn't," she said.

"But please." He smiled.

Tch. Even the waiter's haircut was perfectly feathered up the sides. His cuffs were neat, his suit jacket flawlessly tailored.

In lifting the beautiful flute off the tray, Bronwyn felt something unhinge inside her, swing free.

An odd question popped out of her.

"Colin, do you ever find that what you really love are not ideas but *things*?"

His sandy eyebrows lifted. He leaned in a little closer to hear her better.

"Like your kitchen," she said. "I'm so in love, Colin, I'm so in love . . . with your kitchen."

"You are?" he asked.

"Oh yes," she admitted, somberly. "I am."

And then she saw it: a flicker in his eyes. A slightly wolfish flicker. An "I'm very interested in this conversation" flicker. An "I've got a case of French wine back at my house—would you like to try some?" flicker.

"Well, Bronwyn," he purred, carefully lifting a piece of hair from the side of her mouth. "I never knew."

The idea rose before her in a big champagne thought-bubble: an affair with Colin Martin. God. She could see it.

There would be dinner at places like this every night. There would be oysters, there would be flutes of champagne, there would be murmured conversations in these deep leather booths, the hush of money all around them. There would be gifts of little slippery evening dresses, like the ones all these women were wearing. They would probably have sex all over that house, that enormous Pasadena house. You could probably go from room to room even, totally naked, right there in the middle of the day!

So Colin was interested.

And it might be possible:

Something carnal and elaborate and complicated and secret . . .

And full of tearful whispered phone calls into the night . . .

And the shattering confession . . .

And the terrible bewilderment . . .

And finally Paul's figure hunched over their bed—the slender reed of him finally snapped, utterly broken—his shoulders shaking with silent weeping as she emptied her underwear drawers into a suitcase and . . . oh well.

Bronwyn felt herself sigh, draw her hovering foot back and retreat from the cliff.

"Paul is doing very well," she said, more heavily than she meant to.

"Paul! Sure." His tone was perfectly smooth. "I was going to ask you if you two were still together. Wasn't sure. Ginny hadn't mentioned it."

"Oh yes!" she said, a tad too broadly, comically, her voice almost vaudevillian. "Living together almost seven years!"

"Jeez." He patted her arm, conciliatory, supportive. "Good for you guys. Good for you."

They continued to sip champagne. A boozy silence fell upon them. It was as though they were married conventioneers having that last free Marriott drink of the weekend, suffused with the knowledge that once again, as usual, a flirtatious evening at the bar would end with them trudging companionably up the stairs to their separate bedrooms.

Colin sighed. With slight effort, he heaved himself dutifully at Paul, that third dead weight who had somehow intruded himself into their conversation.

"Paul still writing his . . . great old . . . crazy fiction? Such a great talent," he said.

Here was Bronwyn's opening. She roused herself to it, but cumbersomely, like a cow trying to scramble over a low gate after having eaten too much hay.

"Actually, Paul is working on scripts now . . ."

"Really?"

"Yes—he has made a whole new move into, you know, commercial stuff."

"Why?" He turned to her, quizzical. "So many people wish they had the kind of unique vision Paul does."

"Well," she replied, "he still has that too of course . . ."

"My advice would be . . . stay with novels. You can control them."

"Well, actually, Paul has some great television ideas he has been kicking around."

Colin did not move for a moment.

"Uh-huh," was all he said, noncommittal.

Bronwyn hurled herself in, blind, a body before bullets.

"We were thinking maybe you could look at some of them."

"It's just, Paul is such a terrific, wonderful freethinker . . . Television is so bla and formulaic."

"Well, he knows that, he knows that. Paul isn't naive about that stuff anymore. He's grown up a lot."

"It's just . . ." Colin lifted another glass of champagne off a tray. "The thing is that there *is* a formula. That's the thing. Paul *will* have to conform to a formula."

"It's a formula, yes."

"It's a *formula*," Colin repeated.

Bronwyn had a split-second impression that they were lumbering together like two circus bears in an awkward dance. Somehow she couldn't quite get a toehold.

Just a moment ago Colin had been telling her that television was so below them, so very far below.

But now that she and Paul were trying, ever so lightly, to jump into it, it was an abyss into which Colin simply wouldn't allow them to tumble.

But she was wrong.

"As long as he knows that—and is ready to put up with all the bullshit—sure, sure." Colin's tone was suddenly light again, friendly. "Send it to my office. Anytime."

"Terrific!" Bronwyn beamed.

She had done it! She had done it! She had schmoozed!

"Harold!" Colin exclaimed.

Harold King's smooth face, with its lionlike mane, turned toward Colin.

The handsome blank features were yanked into a smile—but the eyes were guarded. "Do I know you?" the eyes wondered.

Bronwyn held her breath.

When actually face to face with Harold King, the memory of her failure to connect with him at the *LA LA* magazine party gripped her.

Would Colin flop equally?

But no.

"Colin Martin!" Colin exclaimed, tapping his tuxedoed chest. "ABC. Dramatic development—"

Then all at once there was golf talk between Colin and Harold. Laughter. Patting of shoulders. A smooth easiness. Something, Bronwyn noted with a pang, that her own beloved Paul would never be able to do. But never mind.

Harold's face froze again, for just a nanosecond, when he noticed Bronwyn. "Do I have to actually meet this person?" his hesitation seemed to say. "Or can we just sweep on?"

Bronwyn took a breath, and leapt.

"Petra!" Bronwyn cried out, wheeling to her right and giving the slender cream-colored figure a hug. My God she's bony, Bronwyn thought. She felt the slight warning pressure of Colin's hand on her elbow. But she did not care. She did not care. "How good to see you again! How gorgeous you look!"

"Well hello!" Petra replied, smiling, her face a blank.

"We met at a *LA LA* magazine party," Bronwyn chattered on. She felt as though she were flying without a net, yet at the same time oddly elated, like she was hurtling beyond the atmosphere in an electric-blue rocket jet with plush bucket seats and its own speedometer, tachometer . . .

She had schmoozed for Paul, she had schmoozed! And inch by inch, mile by mile, she knew that she could help create a powerful swirl like this around him.

"I think it's so wonderful of you two to have adopted a little girl. I think it's terrific. Although I do hope . . ."

Here Bronwyn leaned forward for the kicker.

"I do hope that motherhood won't keep you away from . . . *designing your exquisite jewelry!*"

It was as though Bronwyn had incanted: "Open sesame!"

Visible relief blew through the group. Figures and faces moved and stirred.

"Of course you won't stop your designing, will you, lamb?" Harold murmured affectionately and somewhat indulgently, as though to a favorite pet.

"Well, I—" Petra began, her cheeks flushed with color.

Champagne-fueled, Bronwyn stood her ground, addressing her remarks to each of them. "No one else is doing what Petra is in L.A. She really has an artist's eye. *Not* like the junk you find at Fred Segal. What are they good for? Tennis tops? Terry-cloth sweatbands?"

At this . . .

Petra King . . .

Who had seemed to grow a full four inches during Bronwyn's speech . . .

Threw back her perfect auburn pageboy, closed her agelessly smooth blue eyes, opened her cream-colored lacy arms wide . . . and that classic, deep-throated chuckle burbled out of her. It was that earthy, patented Petra King Chuckle. It was that Big Chuckle, that chuckle that said, "I am here I am gorgeous I am the queen! I am the queen! I am the queen!"

Colin was looking at Bronwyn with a new, searching look.

"Roger!" Harold suddenly called out, to a short stout balding man in dark sunglasses. His sleeve reached across Colin's face to shake hands with Mr. Next in Line . . .

"Refresh my memory," Petra said, in her newly rich, husky voice, taking Bronwyn's hand in her own smooth, cool one and leading her two steps away from the hub.

"We met at the *LA LA* magazine party? When was that, I wonder?"

"Last December," Bronwyn supplied.

"And that—?" Petra murmured, indicating Colin, who floundered in the background, trying to maintain a gravitational toehold in the nucleus of Armani suits which were slowly trying to spit him out.

"A friend," Bronwyn pronounced flatly. "ABC. Dramatic Series Development. I would have brought my boyfriend, Paul Hoffstead, the screenwriter . . . but these days he's working, working, working. He's never around."

Petra raised her eyebrows in mock dismay. "Tell me about it! Harold just came back from ten weeks on a Tom Selleck movie in Brazil! So," she added kindly, "your Paul—he's doing well?"

"Well . . ." Bronwyn labored to get her tone so right, so casual. "Indeed he is. We're looking into buying a house."

"Kip!" Petra exclaimed. "But you must call my friend Kip!"

"Kip?"

"Kip Tarkanian!" An image rose to Bronwyn's mind—surely not the Kip Tarkanian whose smart red-and-black signs dotted

every third block in L.A.? But of course, these were the Kings—
they were the sort of people who said "Elton" and you knew they
meant "John." "Please call him. Tell him I sent you. He'll help you
find something wonderful, really wonderful.

"Where are you thinking of buying?" At this seemingly casual
question, Petra's face froze into a mask of—of worry.

Oh gosh. Bronwyn's mind moved back to the scene in Colin's
kitchen with lightning speed. There the MTV person stood with
her dreadlocks and green, red, yellow, and black coveralls, raised
one jangling brown wrist, and spoke.

"Definitely not in the Valley!"

"Oh good," Petra murmured, "you don't want to go there. The
Valley is all—all built on shale."

"On what?"

"Shale," Petra declared, wrinkling—or at least trying to—her
brow. "All of the San Fernando Valley is shale, as well as some of
the Hollywood Hills. Below about Barham is fine. But I wouldn't
want to go too much higher than that. The ground, you know . . ."
She tilted her head forward, whispered, "Moves."

"And certainly not anyplace like Echo Park," Bronwyn erupted,
MTV's speech coming back to her in sudden clear chunks. "I really
find it kind of . . ."

"Grimy," they both said at the same time.

Petra broke out into delighted laughter, grabbed her arm. "Isn't
this hysterical? We think the same way! You must call Kip. Call
Kip. He will take care of you." Petra hugged her. "I promise."

"if you lived here,
you'd be home by now!"

Bronwyn excitedly reported to Paul about her successful schmooze evening.

"Isn't that great? Colin said he'll read your stuff at ABC! And also I got the name of a great real estate agent from Petra King! I actually think she is, sincerely, a nice person. I imagine that even Harold would turn out to have good qualities, once one really got to know him—"

Paul didn't say anything for a moment.

"So what do you think you'll send over to him? Colin said he was really, really open to—"

"Noni." Paul looked up at her, somberly, pushing up his Elvis Costello glasses.

"What?"

"The Colin Martin thing . . . I really appreciate your making the effort, sweetie, but it doesn't really mean anything."

Bronwyn was stung.

"What do you mean, it doesn't mean anything?"

"It's . . . That's what I've been trying to tell you. A lot of times when these Hollywood types say, 'Call me,' it doesn't really mean that they want you to call them."

"What are you *talking* about?" Her voice was shrill.

Paul sighed. "It's like . . . In L.A. there are, like, these two tribes of people. There are these big Hollywood people . . ." He put one hand up. "And then there are these kind of, like . . . tattered Bohemians. Us." He put up his other hand, but much lower than the first one.

"I don't consider myself that much lower! I don't—"

"The Hollywood people—like a kind of debauched royalty—they like to keep us Bohemians around like court jesters. Or like pets. They take us out to dinner occasionally and complain about how shallow their work is. We tell them about our brave little performance poetry projects and they say how wonderful we are . . . you know, how idealistic, how creative, how full of integrity, et cetera."

His eyes looked baleful behind his glasses.

"What they really mean to say is . . . 'You're *losers*!' "

Bronwyn recoiled.

Paul shook his head.

"They don't really want to help us. It's like we're this . . . lower class of people. We keep hoping people like Colin Martin will throw us a bone. But they won't. Even though they always say they will. Because actually they think they're better than us. And maybe they are. I don't know."

Bronwyn couldn't believe her ears.

"Paul . . . this is horrible! Don't you think . . . don't you think that maybe you've become just a bit paranoid over the years? You can't even accept an offer of help when it's given to you!"

"It's just . . . Noni, all I am is a writer. A dull writer. I don't dress right. I don't talk right. I don't 'pitch' things. I just write things. I've come to terms with this about myself. I've seen guys who can pitch entire sitcoms based on nothing and get huge deals, and they can't even write word one. I wish it was otherwise, but it's not."

"Don't you think you're being a little . . . self-destructive? A little . . . unreasonable?"

"I just don't get mad at everything anymore."

"But maybe if you could just meet with Colin . . ." she pleaded. "Just once?"

"Noni, a homeless person is more likely to get a movie of the week with ABC. In fact, they *are* likely. Homelessness is, like, a catchy story."

"Don't you want to at least try? You have such great story ideas. You don't want to be doing Zibby Tanaka forever . . ."

But Paul didn't move. He looked out the window, a bit sad.

"The Zibby Tanaka gig is not glamorous, but at least it's real."

The whole conversation left Bronwyn both devastated . . . and horrified. Was this really Paul's plan? To accept only the bad jobs—never try for the good jobs?

Of course, she thought mournfully, it was only because he had been stung so many times before. He had become just so oversensitive.

So, like an animal in the wild, Bronwyn would just have to coax Paul back into civilization. Stack the deck for him a bit, lure him in. She would create the environment around him, the bubble, that would make him attractive to these people. So that her love would not have to worry about any of the bullshit. She would worry about the bullshit. This would free him up to just . . . write.

As for the ABC thing, she began privately copying off some of Paul's old stuff and preparing a packet for Colin Martin.

Poor Paul. He was under so much stress.

"And . . . action!" Henry leaned forward in excitement.

All eyes turned to take one of *Diversity 2000 with Zibby Tanaka*. Studio A at Hanelle Sherwood Films featured a set that looked like the backdrop for one of the better infomercials—pale green walls, pale pink vases holding pale yellow flowers, a pale blue couch and a pale beige coffee table waiting behind.

The Business World: an ocean of pastel, Bronwyn reflected.

The door opened, and out stepped Zibby Tanaka, Diversity Consultant. She was the picture of dapper professionalism with her cap of glossy black hair, large silver button earrings, and smart navy-blue dress suit accented by a magenta and green silk scarf. She smiled into the camera, a massive black behemoth of a thing on a dolly. She had no fear of it.

"As we approach the twenty-first century, demographers predict that the percentage of white males in the workplace will *decrease* . . ." Zibby Tanaka lowered one slightly plump white hand to illustrate. "While the number of minorities—including persons of color, senior citizens, and the otherly abled—will *increase*." Here the neat white hand rose.

"It is this pool of untapped talent," Zibby Tanaka continued, stepping carefully down the stairs as the three cameras dollied in, "a wellspring of exciting new perspectives, skills, experiences, and capabilities . . . that we call *Diversity 2000*."

Zibby Tanaka turned to face the camera on her right.

"Yes. There will be challenges . . ."

At this, a slight cloud crossed Zibby Tanaka's face. No, it was not really a cloud, it was more just a reasonable, pensive look—as though she were simply reminding herself to complete some later task. Not a task, more like a simple errand, something easy, one of many easy errands such as picking up dry cleaning that has already been paid for.

"Certainly *education* is needed. We need to learn about each other's cultural differences. We need to understand each other's backgrounds, each other's sensitivities. The African-American. The senior citizen. The single mother . . .

"Meanwhile, the turbulent nineties have already brought enormous Change to many of America's corporations. Widespread downsizings and rightsizings have brought a sense of living from one day to the next. Fearing and dreading Change is a natural human instinct. Remember, however . . ."

And here she graced her invisible audience with a smile. Not a wide, brainless newscaster smile, but one of great empathy and Communication. Communication was one of Zibby Tanaka's ten "Big C's" of Diversity Training.

What were the others? Bronwyn tried to remember. "Community." "Cooperation." "Caring." They had gone over it together. Bronwyn had *Cliff Note*d the workbook for Paul.

"The Chinese character for Change is a combination of the pictogram for danger . . ."

Zibby Tanaka's face took on a slightly blank look, a patient waiting for such a ridiculous idea to pass on.

"And *opportunity*." On the word "opportunity," Zibby positively dimpled. That was really the word she preferred. "And *opportunity* . . ." She leaned forward. "Is what the time-proven techniques of Diversity 2000 management training will bring to your—"

Zibby Tanaka froze. Squinted into the monitor. Twirled. The magenta and green silk scarf flew out to one side.

"What is *that*?" she shrieked, pointing one of her plump white Diversity 2000 hands.

Bronwyn felt her face go cold. There was a stirring, a murmuring; black shapes around her began jostling against each other like panicked subway passengers.

"Cut!" Henry called out.

An El Pollo Loco box. Someone had left his El Pollo Loco box in the corner of the pastel infomercial stage.

Three crew guys immediately sprang on it, but too late to bring Zibby Tanaka's Confidence, Communication, Caring back. Henry, and Robert Washington and Leif Johnson, the Hanelle Sherwood Films representatives, flocked around Zibby protectively.

"It wasn't even *in* the shot," Henry assured her. "I'll show you. We can roll back the—"

"Not that it should have been left there at all!" Leif Johnson cried out, seizing on a different tack. "I can't believe—"

"You are doing *such* a great job!" Robert enthused, over the top of both. "I swear, Zibby, you are such a natural—"

Zibby held her plump white hands up to shush them all. Her black-lashed, almond-shaped eyes were closed as if, for that moment, she was just too weary to open them. Eyes still shut, she tilted her glossy black cap back as if waiting for cool rain to fall from the heavens. Even her cheerful magenta and green silk scarf seemed to sag a bit.

"Me . . ." When her voice came out it was surprisingly soft, sad, meditative. "It's all on me." She opened her black eyes, fixed them pleadingly on her triumvirate of whipping boys. "Why is it always all on me?"

"Zibby." Robert was jumping in. "The shot was okay—"

Zibby laid her hand on the shoulder of Robert's brown wool jacket. It looked small and frail there. She looked as though only a huge effort was keeping her from bursting into tears. "The stress," she whispered hoarsely, as though Robert was the only one who might even begin to understand. "The stress, Robert. Do you know how much *stress* I'm feeling?"

Oh God, Bronwyn thought. Is this bad for Paul? Is this bad for Paul?

"I know, hon, I know." Robert had one brown arm around Zibby and was speaking to her in a soothing undertone. And she was letting him. Apparently, they had done this together before. Meanwhile, Leif and Henry were looking at each other, frozen.

"I give so much of myself," Zibby declared simply. "Give give give. So much of the time . . ." She tilted her smooth, honey-toned face, fringed by neat black hair and silver buttons, to the lights, as if for the first time understanding a truth about herself.

"I feel that if I am not there, holding the . . . the whole thing together—being here, talking before the camera, making sure the *content* is right, the *content* . . ."

She turned pleadingly to Robert.

"You know how much I care about *content*. I know you guys at Hanelle Sherwood thought the last script was wonderful, but I am an experienced management consultant and I saw *problems*."

She whirled about suddenly.

"This script SUCKS!" she shrieked. "It SUCKS! WHERE is the writer? WHO wrote this script?"

Paul was brought out from the darkness, hustled in front of her. He stood, hunched, like a black crow on the pastel Diversity 2000 set. His face was white.

"Where did you learn to write?" she asked. "This is terrible. So wooden."

"It's straight from the manual," Paul said, in a slightly wobbling voice. "The one you wrote. Which was what I was told to—"

"Are you arguing with me?" Zibby was amazed.

They stood still, facing each other, in a white-hot moment. Bronwyn clutched one icy hand to her neck.

"I . . ." Paul exhaled a big breath, lowering his head. "I will be more than happy to rewrite it—"

"Of course you will be happy! Of course you—"

Zibby turned away from him, pressed her hands to her temples. "Advil. Advil."

"Advil!" Henry cried out, springing to life, his directorial course suddenly clear. He turned to the crew, shading his eyes with his hand. "Advil! Who has Advil?"

Advil. Bronwyn fumbled in her purse. Lipstick. Keys. Datebook. Her fingers scrabbled madly. Save Paul's job. Save Paul's job. Zippered compartment. Pen. Packet of Certs. But no . . . yes! There it was, the slightly crumpled strip of four . . .

"*Advil!*" she shrieked, holding the strip above her as though it were a winning lottery ticket, motoring toward the set. She felt a sense of headiness. "*Advil!*"

Zibby Tanaka lifted her glossy dark head and gazed at Bronwyn.

"This is my girlfriend, Bronwyn Peters," Paul mumbled.

"Advil," Bronwyn repeated.

A smile broke out across Zibby Tanaka, Diversity Consultant's, face. "I love your earrings!" she cried, reaching out for the little Guatemalan doll earrings.

"You can have them!" Bronwyn exclaimed.

Zibby burst into delighted laughter at the ridiculousness of it.

On cue, everyone on the set broke into loud relieved laughter. The tension had broken.

"Of course not," Zibby replied. "But thank you for offering. The writing on this project: so-so," she joked, nudging Paul warmly in the ribs, like a temporarily errant son. "But the accessories . . ." She twinkled, giving a thumbs up.

With a resigned sigh, she turned back to the matter at hand.

"All right. Let's just take five and then try it again, shall we?"

"Thank you, Noni," Paul mouthed to Bronwyn, his face ten different shades of color. "Thank you."

Bronwyn walked down the celadon-colored carpets, past the oak wall paneling, brass-framed etchings, and mahogany desks of Kip Tarkanian Realtors.

Bronwyn had that feeling, once again, that she was in a dream. A dream of hushed tones, deep pile, dark woods. It was the world where money lived.

She would never before have dreamed that this was the kind of place where she would feel comfortable, where she would fit in.

But where did she fit? What did she like? What was hers? What shouldn't be hers?

Last week she had gone into the Onyx Café in Silverlake. This used to be Paul and Bronwyn's favorite place. They'd meet friends there, discuss books, ideas, and records. Going to the Onyx used to make her feel calm and centered.

But to her shock, she realized that the Onyx had become just too grody for her.

Where was the romance?

Out in front were young white guys begging. White guys begging? She didn't remember this. They were like these . . . slacker street kids, twenty-one-year-olds with Rastafarian braids and orange-and-purple knit caps. One had a beat-up guitar which he stroked tunelessly.

Taped to the back of the Onyx cash register were horribly xeroxed flyers for the usual local experimental music bands . . . Gentian, Screamer, Electronic Garbage Box. But instead of having the rebellious energy of teendom, everyone pictured looked forty-five years old and haggard and filthy.

She'd had a mind to get a plate of pasta, just something simple, something cheap, for $7. But it was not to be. To her amazement the food at the Onyx was in fact much, much cheaper than she remembered it and much, much worse. The best she could get was a sloppy bowl of flavorless lentil soup for $1.75 and a huge crust of rock-hard bread. She bit into it and practically cut her lip. As for the bathroom . . . she didn't even want to look.

Bronwyn was just too old to cut her lip on a roll anymore or to sleep on a futon. She had backaches. She couldn't even move her neck in the morning sometimes . . .

"Bronwyn Peters! How good to meet you!"

The final door swung open and there stood Kip Tarkanian, Realtor, rising from behind his mahogany desk. Through the magic of recessed lighting, deep among books and plush chairs, he glowed like an idol.

And why not? Kip Tarkanian, six-foot-two and a trim 180, was the sort of man who grew just ever more magnificent as he strode forward into his forties. His full head of dusky blond hair had the slightest boyish wave—of a man who, while steeped in fiscal responsibility, would obviously not turn down a brisk game of tennis. His strong Harrison Ford–esque features gleamed bronze. His gold wire–rimmed glasses added that something presidential. His black turtleneck coated his lean-waisted torso like the leotard of some kind of superhero.

In fact, the visual cut of the black turtleneck was the one element that stuck out, vibrating faintly, in this otherwise conservative office. Beyond conservative, really. It was so Colonial American you half expected George Washington to come prancing out in his knickers, hoisting the Declaration of Independence. The wallpaper was a celadon and white stripe; the chairs were cherrywood Duncan Phyfe; to the left was a brass-embossed grandfather clock; to the right, some kind of barometer, vaguely nautical with its wheels and dials.

Wheels and dials. Just like Colin Martin's watch. Bronwyn could only wonder at this marvelous new universe, where surfaces sometimes gave way to expose the innards of things—such strange clockworks. Like white bankers' legs on Lifecycles, churning away.

"Bronwyn!" Kip exclaimed again, grasping her hand. Confidence flowed from him, strengthening her. "I think we're going to be able to do something very nice for you. Very nice." He motioned her to sit in a Duncan Phyfe chair, posing his own taut behind lightly on the edge of his mahogany desk. His movements were faintly catlike. "Coffee?"

"Coffee sounds good," Bronwyn admitted, feeling oddly humble. "I'm trying to quit, but I'd love just a small cup."

The magnificent head tilted to look out the door. His expression suddenly went into this cool, appraising, dead-eyed look. It was the look of a person diverting their attention from royalty in order to snap their fingers and rattle off quick commands for subservient help.

Boy would Paul be surprised to see this, Bronwyn thought.

"Lisa?" Kip's eyes slid back to Bronwyn. "Cream and sugar?"

"Oh, yes."

He winked. "Just like me. An abuser. You got it, babe."

The obsequious Lisa appeared, a pale blond twenty-three-year-old whose face had no striking features whatsoever. In her white sweater and pale gray skirt, she was as close to wallpaper as a person could be. Only her gray eyes glittered slightly, with restless internhood, behind her tortoiseshell rims.

"Lis', two coffees, cream, sugar—and did the appraisal on the Yamamoto property come in yet?"

Yamamoto. The Japanese. Of course: the Japanese and Los Angeles real estate. Kip Tarkanian must make deals like this all the time. Bronwyn felt sly, as though she was looking directly into the wheels and dials of big business.

"Three o'clock." Lisa made the slightest obeisance when she said this. A nanosecond later—in a poof, almost—she was gone.

"Bronwyn." Kip put both hands up, looked away as though trying to focus his words. Bronwyn found herself following his gaze as he took in the celadon wallpaper, the grandfather clock, the large paned windows flanked by heavy pale brocade curtains, the dark wood bookshelves basking under muted track lighting. All at once, faintly, the grandfather clock began to chime.

At this chiming he put his hands down, laughed, relaxed, shook his golden head. "It's been crazy around here."

"Really!" Bronwyn exclaimed. She felt as though she had been looking at the very picture of serenity. The rich, she thought. The rich. Their craziness is not like our craziness.

The words flowed out of him, melodiously, along their own well-modulated grooves. "My God! The week we've had. I closed two properties Monday, went into escrow on another on Tuesday, listed another just today—beautiful cottage, three bedrooms, one and a half baths, gorgeous rose garden, solarium to die for, Mexican tile, Frank Gehry design but with *land*. Very rare. Already I've had eight broker calls on the place."

Our Frank Gehry cottage.

Bronwyn instantly saw the perfection of it: herself and Paul puttering around in the sun-swept bungalow, rosebushes bobbing outside, spots of color against bright green grass. Above: the veranda, in latticed white trelliswork like from some Impressionist painting.

"Where is it?" Bronwyn asked, quickly, longingly, before she could stop herself.

"Above Los Feliz," Kip replied. His face was still flushed with the magic of the house, but his voice tinkled with just a hint more coolness. "It's listed for one point four million."

As quickly as her desire had lunged out from her, she retracted it. Over your head! Over your head! a voice inside her screamed. Red alarm lights flashed and submarine men hurried in panic to their posts.

One point four million! Kip Tarkanian Realtors would certainly demand their coffee back, as they ushered her out. Get out! Get out! Back to the parking lot! But there were so many celadon-and-walnut Kip Tarkanian offices to run through: she would get lost. Better to melt into the carpet, leaving no trace, one last whisper on her lips: "I'm sorry—sorry to have wasted your time. I thought we were here to buy real estate, but actually we can't afford it."

Because in one fell swoop, their $26,000—her amulet—had shrunk to a greasy table scrap. And so . . . had she.

It was as if he could read her mind.

"What kind of down payment are you thinking about, Bronwyn?" Kip Tarkanian, Professional, cut in quietly.

The question hung in the flat air.

Not knowing what else to do, Bronwyn Peters, imposter, uttered what she now realized was an obscenity. "Twenty-six thousand."

Kip Tarkanian's face betrayed no change, no movement.

His voice continued, perfectly measured, impossible to read. "Los Feliz is a little beyond *our* price range then—"

"Of course, of course," Bronwyn protested, her face flaming hot. "I don't know what I was—"

"As twenty percent of one point four million puts you in the three-hundred-thousand down payment range," he said gently.

What had she been thinking? Frank Gehry design? Rose garden? Los Feliz? She was insane! Insane! She should be whipped, punished, made to sit in a corner wearing a conical hat. Was he going to slap her? Call security guards? Press a button behind his desk, causing a trapdoor to open and swallow her?

Kip Tarkanian did none of these things.

Amazingly, his eyebrows lifted, allowing a little sunshine to slip in.

"A year ago," he mused, as though considering an abstract philosophical tenet, "you wouldn't have been able to get anything in the L.A. basin for twenty-six. However . . ."

He lifted a hand. And then . . . the hand tilted, just slightly.

Bronwyn could tell something of enormous import was being conveyed by that tilting hand.

"Since the Gulf War, the market has slowed. People are just a little more cautious. Prices are no longer going up, up, up."

Kip leaned in toward her. His eyes crinkled. They were a team again, two coffee abusers, yakking about real estate. "There are bargains out there. Major bargains."

Bronwyn felt a tiny wave of hope splashing over her. "There are?" she whispered.

"There are." Kip leaned back. The tilting hand dropped casually away, taking its major bargains with it. "But you have to move quickly," he added almost callously. "These prices aren't going to be around forever. You have to seize the moment. You can't wait around. The Southern California real estate market is going to bounce right back up . . ."

As he continued speaking, Bronwyn felt herself cautiously climbing back onto the wagon, the real estate wagon. As she did, finding her seat, steadying herself, she felt herself catching some of his callousness—callousness toward the footdraggers, the lolly-gaggers, the naysayers. Them. The people who were going to miss this quick opening he was describing—this pause for breath in the climb of the real estate market . . .

This Gulf War bobble in home prices was like the brief parting of the Red Sea. And Kip Tarkanian was Charlton Heston in a turtleneck. She and Paul, hysterically driving their mules, baskets flying, could seize the moment and quickly race to the other side . . . the homeowner side. But they must do so fast.

"So you think we could get something—even with our small down payment?" she persisted. She just wanted to make sure all the hatches were battened down before the tropical monsoon of pie-in-the-sky real estate fantasizing came down.

"Almost," Kip said carefully, putting the warding-off hand back up. Like a small terrier tossed a morsel of chicken, then told to stay off the bed, Bronwyn felt her shoulders and torso cringing in a posture of abject subservience, to communicate more completely the conscious negation of her will.

"Every other person who walks in this office asks for West Hollywood, Brentwood, Venice, whatever," he declared, falling boyishly into his cavernous leather chair. "And I say, 'Great.' The Westside is great. I love the Westside. Who doesn't want to live there? You've got restaurants, shops, Montana Avenue, the beach." But the way he rattled these off was slightly tired, as if to say, "But L.A. is so much more than that, isn't it?"

Bronwyn thought wistfully of the Westside. Even though she sensed where this was going: Kip Tarkanian was somehow not going to allow her and Paul to live there.

"We do business there like crazy. Three-mil, three-point-five-mil homes." He made a hilarious, dismissing motion with his hand. "My commissions are through the roof. I went to frigging Brazil last Christmas, for God's sake! Took three weeks off! Didn't hesitate a second! Life is good, knock wood." He did knock on his desk—clock, clock, clock—for good measure.

"Bronwyn." He repeated her name again. Every time he said it, she felt like she was being jerked one inch closer to him, as though he held her by a string attached to her breastbone. "I could sell you some tiny place in the Westside for top, top dollar. Actually, probably I couldn't." He glanced at a folder in passing. "Not for a down payment of twenty-six thou.

"The most sensible thing—the best *investment* for the price, if that's your main concern . . ." He took a heavy pause. "Would be to go to the Valley."

Bronwyn felt the G-force smear everything around her into hallucinogenic, neon, *2001*-style ribbons.

"No-o-o!" The word tore out of her. "No. No. Absolutely not. Not the Valley!"

"Now the Valley is very reasonable," he murmured, as though toying dangerously with the shoulder strap of her slip, presaging a dastardly move neither wanted to make, that both would definitely regret in the morning. "Three-bedroom houses. Add-on family rooms. Two car garages. Flat land. Family-oriented housing. Bread-and-butter stuff. Not much view, not much style, but you can't go wrong in terms of resale."

"No," Bronwyn whispered. "No."

"Most brokers would counsel that to you, in your price range," he persisted. He picked up his Bible-size computer-printout listing book, flipped casually through. He opened it to a random page, snapping the binder back to hold it open. "For instance, here. Look at this. A cute little two plus one starter home in . . . Reseda."

Reseda. The death knell.

" 'Cape Cod style.' Nice—though unfortunately they do mean faux Cape Cod," he added pityingly.

Faux Cape Cod. The most hideous perversion of her old New England dream.

"Aboveground pool. That means Doughboy. That means blue plastic and chain-link fence. Here's a photo. A lot of cement lining the backyard, it's true.

"But a sensible deal." He arranged his features into a calm, reasonable demeanor. "A very sensible place to build equity. I know brokers who would—"

"No," Bronwyn whispered. "Not the Valley. No."

"You realize that most Realtors would show you the door right now."

Grimly, Bronwyn gripped her Duncan Phyfe chair. She had already been totally humiliated. She had laid herself open for him. And now she wasn't leaving without a bone. She had slogged her way too far through this exhausting conversation.

"There is another option," he revealed, after a moment.

Bronwyn did not trust herself to speak, to break the spell.

A mug of coffee appeared in her hand. A plate of chewy oatmeal cookies—their chunks rugged, earthen, and deeply good, making one think words like "crockery"—was slipped between them, at snatching distance. "Thank you," Kip mouthed at Lisa, sending a tiny jolt of electricity her way. Lisa pushed her colorless head down in an uncomfortable, impossible-to-read expression and twisted out of the room again.

"Something cosmopolitan. Great location. Great investment. You don't want the Westside. The market there's all played out. You're on the cutting edge—you want a place with a future. But a home that's absolutely perfect now."

"Yes," she breathed.

"Downtown."

"Downtown?" At first the words make no impression on her.

But then she remembered—the spears, the glass, the towers.

Tomorrowland.

Downtown: the Future.

The banner floated back to her: "IF YOU LIVED HERE, YOU'D BE HOME BY NOW!"

"We could buy down there?"

He just laughed.

Kip pushed a video into the mahogany console, dimmed the lights with one quiet touch.

A trumpet fanfare greeted her. "Dump duh duh duh!" From across a brilliant blue sky—the very stratosphere—a shining logo came spinning. "The Los Angeles Visitors Bureau!" a deep man's voice exclaimed, and then . . .

"COME HOME TO DOWNTOWN!"

Easy jazz—the saxophone player feeling good, if slightly funky, slightly frisky (as befitted a forward-looking city)—propelled the viewer forward as the camera winged along in the fresh blue air above Los Angeles, a latticework of stately green palms, pastel Art Deco boulevards, glittering swimming pools. Sleek cars moved easily along its thoroughfares.

"Tail of the Pup" zipped by, Marilyn's painted face simpered on a wall, a male and a female Rollerblader in matching neon Crystal Lite outfits did a twirl and waved, three laughing teenage girls— hair teased, matching lime-green sunglasses—collapsed together in the back of their red convertible, laughing. Greatly amused by the scene, and obviously not a little charmed as well, the bass player came to a sudden playful pop, then returned to the gentle samba groove.

"Dynamic, vibrant, colorful," the man continued, "Los Angeles has always been a mecca for those seeking relaxed, sophisticated living. The glitter of Hollywood, the call of Southern California's beautiful beaches, the family fun of Anaheim's Magic Kingdom"—here Mickey Mouse waved a white glove, then fell back into the stiff, silent heaving that was the universal sign of mascot-head mirth—"each year over four million visitors come to the City of Angels."

The picture shifted to office workers typing at computer terminals in sleek offices; "Hello!" a fortyish Caucasian businessman greeted two smiling Japanese businessmen; inside an enormous warehouse, a crew of men in orange coveralls and safety goggles waved a crane onto a jet plane in the making. "Hughes Aircraft," it said on the side.

"With Los Angeles' booming economy—not to mention perfect year-round weather and all the amenities of a world-class capital—more and more visitors find they are staying. It's a trend that promises to continue: the business forecast for the nineties, in an increasingly global economy, is unlimited growth. And where they're staying, in increasing numbers, is Downtown."

Rising crisply out of the easy-listening jazz miasma came the opening chords of George Gershwin's Concerto in F, played on triumphal piano. The camera was suddenly now winging eastbound along the 10 Freeway, the shards and angles and towers of downtown's skyscrapers—the view she loved—rising like a vision above the undulating palm trees and speeding cars and collapsing-in-laughter blond teenage girls of the Los Angeles basin.

"At the hub of it all, Downtown is a smart, sophisticated urban center that rivals that of other world capitals. Situated in prime position on the Pacific Rim, it is a magnet for domestic and foreign investment business concerns."

Revealed within the skyscraper mélange were the beetling glass elevators of the Bonaventure Hotel, the blow-dried haircuts of crisp-suited businessmen and women pounding up and down the boulevards amid jostling leather briefcases, shiny escalators zig-zagging up into downtown's granite canyons.

"International travelers enjoy Downtown's first-class hotels, five-star restaurants, and world-class theater. From the Dorothy

Chandler Pavilion to the Ahmanson to the Shubert, classical music lovers and Broadway aficionados can get their fill of top-flight entertainment."

Images of symphony orchestras and opera singers fell away to a neon sign which read, in fast curves of the type written on mirrors in lipstick: "Spa Downtown."

"Spa Downtown!" Bronwyn cried out in amazement. "But— but we were there! The *LA LA* magazine party!"

"Ah." Kip nodded his head. "Good."

The camera angle widened to reveal sophisticated clubbies lining up to get into a ritzy-looking spa, flanked by a phalanx of bouncers in Armani suits. BMWs were pulling up, men with ponytails in leather jackets on Harleys. Blond babes with sprayed hair, in tight red minidresses, loped across the street, throwing their heads back and laughing.

She thought she recognized some of the people, the outfits. They must have filmed this the very night they'd been there.

"For the affluent young set, Downtown is *the* place for nightlife. Trend-setting venues such as the world-famous Spa Downtown— health club by day, nightclub by night—stay open until two." Cut to a flickering screen showing *Entertainment Tonight* interviewing Malcolm Forbes, in his trademark kilt. "Cutting-edge magazines such as *LA LA* keep readers abreast of what's hot. For the confident young professional who has a taste for smart, sophisticated living, this is the place to be."

The coincidence was too much. Bronwyn had a sense of Destiny, a Destiny she was moving toward, on oiled gears, as along the inner concourses of a futuristic freeway.

Fade to a dramatically lit, paint-splotched canvas in a ritzy loft. The shot widened to reveal sophisticated art-lovers in turtlenecks, swirling glasses of white wine, contemplating the artworks and chatting. Outside a huge picture window, the lights of the city glittered against the jet-black night sky like gems.

"It is in Downtown too where the creative spirit of Los Angeles lives and breathes, generating the exciting new artworks of tomorrow."

The screen cut to a handsome Latino man, high forehead, lock of black hair waving forward, somewhat preppily dressed. He sat at a sleek desk in front of the downtown skyscape. "Jorge Santos, Director of the Los Angeles Civic Arts Foundation," the letters flashed underneath.

"Los Angeles is a future-oriented city," Santos said passionately, "that is stepping forward to becoming the premier art center of the nation in the nineties. We are moving away from the staid Eurocentrism of the East Coast. The Pacific Rim is the wave of tomorrow.

"You don't just see this in established centers like MOCA and the County Museum. Downtown is alive with five hundred and twenty-five artist's lofts, at last count, and bustling theater venues like the Los Angeles Theatre Center and the OtherVoices Performance Complex. Different cultures and different generations are coming together in our city to spark a dynamic change in the way we think about art and culture-making."

"And at the center of all of this—theaters, restaurants, museums—is Symphony Towers," the narrator agreed. "At Symphony Towers, you have every amenity today's busy young professional could want, all in one place. A world class health spa. Private shuttles to nearby theaters, museums. Subscriptions to such cutting-edge publications as *LA LA* magazine. The whole diversity of sophisticated, smart L.A. life—it's right here at your doorstep!

"Welcome to Downtown!"

"Welcome to the future!"

The jazz music came up again, and the camera went, in soft focus, to a vision of white gleaming tile, sparkling chrome, light gray granite countertops, recessed track lighting, inset butcher-block cutting boards.

Bronwyn rubbed her eyes. But yes: there were the hanging copper pans, the skylights.

It was . . . her kitchen.

A slim blonde who looked like she had just changed, at the end of her tough working day, into polo shirt and stonewashed jeans moved easily from the Sub-Zero refrigerator to the stove. Through the door behind her, other guests were visible, sipping white wine from fluted glasses, tossing their heads with easy laughter.

"Come home to Symphony Towers," he invited again. "Luxury condos from two hundred and thirty-nine thousand dollars. Come home to Downtown, and *live*."

A map popped up on the screen, with a red arrow pointed to Downtown.

And Bronwyn saw it.

Los Angeles was indeed a city with a heart, a core, a geographical center.

This center was not where Colin Martin was in Pasadena.

Not where Hanelle Sherwood Films was in Hollywood.

Not even where Petra King was in Santa Monica.

It was in Downtown. Downtown was the center, the hub of all freeways.

Downtown was where they could all unite.

"It's a *little* beyond what you have to spend. But"——here Kip narrowed his eyes in that appraising way, a military general about to strategize a campaign—"I think we can get it down. I think we can get it down. If we go for a ten percent down payment instead of a twenty. I have a mortgage broker who can do wonders. We'll do a five-year adjustable. It can be done. Time"—he leaned forward, giving her another pearl—"is on your side."

immaculate

concepción

And so they did it. Bronwyn and Paul bought a condo at Symphony Towers.

Paul was opposed to the idea at first: he thought they should opt for land. But they had lived in Tujunga such a long time—by Paul's choice—that he conceded it was time for Bronwyn to have her way in something.

"But isn't it a problem that we're not married?" he threw in, stalling one last time.

Not at all. Indeed, as Kip Tarkanian pointed out, in California being married was actually a tax disadvantage.

And so it was in the world of business, the world Bronwyn was bringing them into now, finally, for the benefit of both. Kip Tarkanian's offices had given Bronwyn helpful charts and statistics and reports on everything, along with countless computer print-outs and geo maps of the area. There was backup evidence for everything.

Eventually, Paul was won over.

Besides, not even the loan process was painful. Kip referred them to Trey Campbell, a mortgage broker. With his help, they managed to put down their $26,000, including fees and points, securing an astronomical loan.

In truth, Bronwyn had been slightly embarrassed about the loan. It was called an "EZ Qualifier"—which brought to mind someone poor buying a used car from a guy named Shecky. On the other hand, the terms were great. Unlike other loans, you did not have to show official income tax returns to get it, you just filled out forms and solemnly assured the bank you made "enough."

"Everyone's doing it this way," Trey assured her. "It's a snap."

And in fact, the EZ Qualifier was the only way they'd been able to swing it. They couldn't afford a fixed-rate loan with its stern, unforgiving terms. The EZ Qualifier, however, as its name suggested, kind of came halfway to you. It started you off easy, with manageable payments, swelling alarmingly over five years, at which point the whole thing burst, like a boil, into an enormous balloon payment.

But by that time, Paul's income would be such that these things would be no problem.

And in the meantime, they had *this*! She loved *this*!

Bronwyn stood behind the granite island of her white, skylit kitchen, which opened into their calm, white, L-shaped living room. With its high ceilings, pristine walls, and floor-to-head picture windows, it brought to mind the cool upper deck of an ocean liner. An ocean liner moving in stately progress past the gleaming high-rises of downtown L.A.

At the high-rises' very spires were bold neon signs: "Sanyo," Bronwyn read to her left, and then in succession, "Sumitomo," "Wakai," "Toshiba." You almost wanted to be wearing deck shoes and a white cap.

Along the L shape, sunlight spilled over the pearly gray Berber carpet. "Berber carpet." Her lips curved around the phrase, as if it were a code word penthouse dwellers whispered to each other. In the corners were brass Art Deco wall sconces. Up above was that recessed lighting she loved. Everything around her was cool, gleaming, modern: every switch, every latch, every button, motored things along—hatches opened, lights glowed on—with a soft, reassuring click.

The people who lived in Symphony Towers had been great too. You could not wish for more soft-spoken, more responsible neighbors. You instantly felt you could trust them with your keys, your children, your tax returns.

In fact, sometimes Bronwyn wondered if she and Paul were good enough to meet her neighbors' standards.

Fred and Lita, to the left side of the hall, were in advertising— he an executive, she a graphic artist. But Lita, though her "look" drew largely from her hennaed buzz cut and black leggings, was not a struggling artist. She was the type with corporate accounts and a black BMW. Lita tended to keep to herself as she went about her business, carrying up groceries, beeping her car alarm, going to the gym. Though friendly, she often looked a bit abstracted and blank in casual conversation.

Bronwyn approved of this. She did not think graphic artists should be too effusive. She did not think they should leap up in the middle of a conversation and pace about a room, catlike, enthusing about light and color and shape. Too often when they did, as Bronwyn had discovered in the past, in her and Paul's old Bohemian life, it was because they were desperately trying to get you to hire them to do something because they were penniless.

Lita, on the other hand, was free enough from the financial

catfights of life to not have to view every acquaintance as a potential client. This gave Lita the ease of mind to be apathetic, vacant, and even a bit dull. Which meant, to Bronwyn, not desperate . . . and therefore cool.

On the other side of the hall were finance people—finance people, who knew what *that* meant—Hal and Chris. They were decidedly racquetball-playing and Teutonic. Chris especially, with her short-cropped blond hair, pursed lips, lean tennis figure, and beige linen business suits. Bronwyn was a bit afraid of Chris, as Chris was the president of the Condo Association.

Bronwyn did not quite understand about the Condo Association. All she knew was that every so often a neatly typed sheet of pink paper would be slipped under their door. These were Condo Association meeting minutes. Apparently, in some nameless room, the five representatives of the Condo Association met and voted on things—garage door repair, earthquake proofing, estimates on a new intercom service, etc.

She was quite glad there were responsible people doing this, but had the faint sense that she and Paul were being excluded.

Not that she herself had the remotest interest in meeting Thursday nights to discuss garage door repair and earthquake proofing. On the other hand, one wondered why one had not been invited. Who had voted these people in, anyway?

It was a kind of Catch-22. It was like envying your high school's student body government officials for being popular enough to win elections. Even though all they seemed to discuss, once in office, were things like "litter."

But perhaps it was Bronwyn herself who should make the effort. Perhaps she should throw herself into the swing of life at

Symphony Towers—get involved, get active, join committees, sign up.

"Hello! I'm Katy," a pert twentyish blonde greeted Bronwyn at the door. She had a neat cap of hair, a USC-perfect complexion and teeth, and a tidy blue suit. "You're here for the Networking Breakfast?"

"I am," Bronwyn assented.

"Great!" Katy beamed. "Come right this way!"

Conference room C was toward the back of the labyrinth of special Spa Downtown meeting rooms, serene in their pastel carpets and pink and green chevron–patterned wallpaper. Beyond the walls one could hear the vague echo of racquetball play, the little rubber balls hitting against the wall, the distant grunts of players.

"Bronwyn . . . Peters?" When Bronwyn nodded, Katy checked it off with an energetic dash of the pen.

"Help yourself to a cup of coffee and some fruit or Danish." Katy stepped aside to reveal a conference table with a small bouquet of flowers in the middle. Spa Downtown pads and pencils waited neatly in front of each chair. About a dozen or so professionals—looking reassuringly tony in their dark suits and salon-fresh haircuts—stood about, holding cups of coffee, chatting. The skin was burnished, tight, the bellies flat; smiles came easily and naturally.

Standing now in conference room C, Bronwyn once again felt the Hush of Money around her, the easy, relaxed shoulders and fit torsos the very carriages of success.

She felt a stab of nerves.

But then she thought to herself: What did she have to be ashamed of? They were at Symphony Towers. Paul worked for Hanelle Sherwood Films. They drove a Geo Futura. They had a maid, for God's sake.

She pushed her shoulders back with renewed determination.

"Well hello . . ." A cute if somewhat short Italianate young man in flawless double-breasted suit leaned in to look at her name tag. "Bronwyn!" He stuck out his hand. "How are you doing? Name's Tony! Tony Ricci!"

"Hello Tony!" Bronwyn replied.

Tony slipped a card into her hand. "Teddy bears!" he exclaimed, winking at her as though they both shared a private joke. "Teddy bears! You call Tony for your teddy bear needs!"

"Wha—?" Bronwyn still smiled, trying to get with it. Just as she looked down at the card, she felt a hand clap on her shoulder. She turned.

"Bronwyn Peters!" a tall sandy-haired fellow in heavy black Porsche glasses and a velour running suit bellowed. "Jim. Jim Diamond! Diamond Cellular Phone!"

"Well hello!" she exclaimed.

"What cellular phone company are *you* currently using?" he inquired, blond eyebrows arched.

"Well . . . none," she admitted. Not that she wanted to sound too dull, lame, poor. "But I'm definitely thinking of—"

"What line of work you in, Bronwyn?" Jim Diamond persisted, furrowing his brow.

"I'm in—uh, the humanities. Sort of. I was. I'm interested in getting more into the—uh, into the business field, I think . . ."

Jim Diamond's face loomed closer, and therefore larger. Bronwyn now noticed that he had a small gold earring on his left earlobe, hair curling out the top of his running suit, he'd nicked himself shaving that morning on his splotchy reddish neck, and he smelled faintly of some type of cologne splash. It was a lot of detail to take in at seven-fifteen A.M.

"Well, why don't you have a cellular phone, Bronwyn Peters? Do you know how much business you're missing? People are very busy today. Ve-ry busy! Boom boom boom boom boom! Clients are calling! They want this! They want that!"

As his monologue went on, all Bronwyn could think of was how much she longed to be a part of that word "business." What *was* business exactly? What did businesspeople do? All she knew was they wore suits and worked in pastel offices and flew places. Sounded fine to her.

"Business." She found herself bouncing on his flow. "That's my interest. Entrepreneurship," she threw out. "Marketing."

"Bronwyn?" A worried-looking, birdlike blond woman to her left reached for her hand. Bronwyn saw huge blue eyes looking at her through huge round glasses. "Sally Sanders? Ophthalmology?"

Katy rapped on the conference table and commanded their attention. Everyone slugged down their last swallows of coffee, taking their places.

"People?" she declared. "It's seven twenty-five."

Some hurried to sit next to their favorite pal, some held their bodies relaxed, aloof, letting the seating fall where it may. Sometimes randomly letting the cards fall where they may was the key to good Networking, Bronwyn deduced. When one's new neighbor-to-be took a seat, the seated person would turn with a show of surprise and interest, shaking the new person's hand, flashing a business card, raising eyebrows, leaning forward to get the name right.

"I'm just passing out these last-minute Condo Association memos," Katy threw out. "You can save them for later."

And there they were, coming around, another set of pink sheets.

"Another day, another condo memo," someone groaned.

Bronwyn took one and started to stick it into her neat manila folder, but as she was doing so, a phrase at the top caught her eye, printed in bold:

OIL SPOTS

"Business is great," Jim Diamond, the cellular phone king was declaring to the group. He stood easily, almost pleasurably, in his velour running suit, one hip thrust out, casually taking swigs of his decaf as though he were on the back of one of his apparently many yachts. "Absolutely great."

"That's great," a software marketer named Phil put forward. "Because this hasn't been a particularly good time for the personal electronics market."

Upon hearing this, Jim Diamond of Diamond Cellular tilted back his head and narrowed his eyes. Not one whit of pleasure seemed to leave him. His voice remained easy, smooth. "It's true that sales are down a bit, with the economy. Radiation scare didn't help us either." He guffawed suddenly, playing the room, sandy eyebrows arched.

But then he leaned back, rubbing his stomach comfortably.

"Fortunately—and I sure don't need to tell *you* folks this— Diamond Cellular has the only on-site repair facility in town! We're the only people that offer that! The only ones. It's a full-repair facility. So check us out," he invited, passing his business cards along. "You'll like us. Tell 'em Jim sent you . . .

"Because," he reiterated, "we are doing just great, just great! No problems here!"

Heart pounding, Bronwyn's gaze shot down to the memo:

It has come to our attention that occasionally some of the tenants of Symphony Towers may be experiencing a problem with Oil Spots under their vehicles in the parking garage. In fact, there is a very easy and inexpensive solution: Carter's Premium Gravel, available at Builder's Emporium for about $4.99 a can, may be poured upon the problem areas to soak up excess stains . . .

Tony the teddy bear guy had his whole spiel rehearsed, practically to the smallest flutter of his lashes. When he stood, his small feet planted wide apart, his chest spreading in his double-breasted suit, he himself seemed to take on an endearing teddy bear quality. He whipped out a shopping bag full of . . .

"Teddy bears," he confided, leaning forward, a dimple in his cheek, both brown eyes atwinkle. "It's a great business. A great business. Think about it. Who doesn't love teddy bears?"

He spread out his hands as though to emphasize the question.

"No one!" the other networkers chorused, warm hearty laughter bubbling out of them. "No one!"

"You see!" he replied, shooting a finger out, teasing them. "What'd I tell you?"

"Oh gosh." Katy was convulsed with giggles. She was turning red. "Tony, you are a card! You are a card, Tony!"

"Teddy bears," he intoned again, this time a little more darkly, a little more profoundly, as though alluding to some kind of sacred grail. "We're making money hand over fist. And you know why? You know why?"

"Why?" the group asked.

"Versatility!" Tony replied smartly. "Think about it. Consumers go wild. It's the hottest thing on the market. You can use them as a gift"—he pulled a yellow Fred Hayman teddy bear out of the bag—"or as a souvenir!"—up came a gray Hard Rock Café teddy bear. "See?" He reiterated. "Gift"—yellow bear—"or souvenir!"—gray bear. "Gift"—yellow bear—"or souvenir!"—gray bear.

Bronwyn took a moment to laugh with the others, but then her gaze shot back down to the memo:

While your space is certainly your own, we would just like to remind all Symphony Towers tenants that Oil Spots may constitute a potential fire hazard. In addition, please bear in mind that in courtesy to others, we should all strive to keep the common area SANITARY and ATTRACTIVE for all users.

"I've been in Networking groups for six years," a mousy-looking guy named Richard with dark mustache and receding hairline was telling them. "What's exciting for me is that recently I've been invited to head my university alumni association. It's been great in terms of enabling me to keep my networking going. Networking is something that takes time and effort, you get out what you put in, some people don't understand that. They don't know how to network. It really takes practice. By the way, I specialize in financial innovation. For instance, when companies go public—I can facilitate that transition. Okay? Give me a call.

Hey, speaking of Networking, my company is looking to hire—that's right, we're *hiring*." He took a beat, gave an impressive look around. "A controller with at least three to five years' experience, hopefully in the estate-planning area because . . ."

Oil Spots.

Could it be that their Geo Futura . . . was leaking? No. The car was practically new. It couldn't be Bronwyn and Paul that the Condo Association memo was referring to. No. They were clean. Of course.

All eyes turned to Bronwyn. It was her turn to speak.

She stood up, smoothed her skirt, broke into a shaky smile.

"My name is Bronwyn Peters—it's my first Networking Breakfast. I have to apologize—I was very nervous about coming—I'm nowhere near as experienced at this as, say, Richard, who really impressed me! Six years! That's fantastic!"

"Well . . . *welcome*!" exploded Katy. "Good for you! A first-timer!"

"Welcome!" everyone cried out, a sea of warm faces and interested looks and support. "Welcome, Bronwyn!"

Bronwyn felt a ray of hope. Everything was going to be fine.

"The fact is," she pushed on, "until recently I was pursuing my Ph.D. in Women's Studies at UCLA. And that was going very well, very well. I was on scholarship—full ride—the whole nine yards. I've always been very good at academia. So why did I leave, right?"

She fixed her gaze on the pastel wall opposite. The question hung in the air in front of her. On the serving table stood a glass pitcher of water. It shook slightly at each whap! whap! whap! of the racquetball game above them.

It would be so easy to just tell the truth. To unburden herself. To let the sentences tumble forward—that her scholarship had been cut off, that she had been sending out résumés, that she couldn't locate her interest in the subject anyway, that she was worried about Paul's job, that she was worried about their loan . . .

But these people reeked of success. They were kind—but very Professional. They were businesspeople. Real businesspeople. Not imposters like her.

How she longed to just break down and admit that she was totally lost here.

But it seemed that she could never do that in L.A. She always had to keep up the mask.

"I think . . ." She struggled with the words. "I think I'm ready for a transition. A transition. Yes. I guess . . . over the past three years, my academic research has not been quite as fulfilling to me. It has lost some of its excitement. It has become routine."

Routine! How she would love a routine. I drive the BMW to work, make another $1,000, go home, eat my pesto dinner, fall asleep in front of the TV.

"I hear you," an accountant named Pamela called out to her. "My ex-husband was a lawyer and it was the same thing. He could do it by rote after a while."

"Yes," Bronwyn repeated, stiff as a Rose Queen, turning slowly to Pamela, picking up momentum. "Academia has been terrific. It has been great. I certainly can't complain. It's just that our life has become so orderly. You know. You do your research. You teach. You get new grants. You have your flexible vacations. Here Paul and I own a beautiful condo in Symphony Towers—"

"Nice!" Katy chirped up immediately. "Very nice!"

"Although given how we had to rush to buy it, it sometimes amazes me how many condos still seem empty." Bronwyn laughed. "I'm not sure how prices are going to skyrocket if . . ."

A perceptible chill fell in the room.

"But no," Sally the ophthalmologist murmured. "Chris of the Condo Association was just telling me about a huge wait list."

"That's right," said Jim Diamond, the cellular phone king. "All kinds of people are trying to buy in."

"But of course they are!" Bronwyn rushed in. "Of course they are! And Paul and I—Paul's a screenwriter—we love it!"

"He's a writer?" Katy asked.

"Sure. Writes a lot of TV scripts, film scripts," Bronwyn said hurriedly.

"Nice!" Rosalie, a big blonde in real estate, congratulated her. There was happy murmuring. Like some kind of sci-fi effect, Bronwyn felt the rift in the Networking universe closing up again.

"So anyway," Bronwyn finished. "Um, thank you. Carry on."

She sat down, cheeks flushed in embarrassment—but paradoxically felt many hands reaching over to grasp her arm, squeezing it. As though she were not, in fact, a loser. Business cards were flying toward her—

"Oh! Your card!" Katy cried out.

"Oh yes!" the group agreed.

"I . . . will get one," Bronwyn promised, lamely.

There was a burst of laughter.

One happy family again.

Next came Tish and Nurlene. Nurlene looked to be in her forties, fairly overweight, winged yellow Farrah Fawcett hair, large gold hexagonal glasses on a chain, bright pink stretch pants suit over a white ribbed sweater, powder-blue eyeshadow, koala pinned to the lapel. Nurlene's daughter, Tish, was Nurlene minus about twenty years, minus the koala (she boasted a miniature snowman instead).

They were sort of like the Judds, with their mother/daughter duality and their flowing gold hair, but a bit heavier.

But above all of this, their chief distinguishing characteristic was that they were always laughing. In fact, laughing turned out to be their business. It was practically scripted.

NURLENE: Laughterobics! (Nurlene broke into huge peals of merriment, barely able to contain herself.) Changed . . . my . . . life!

TISH: Sounds great . . . (hands spread apart, eyebrows raised) But what is it?

NURLENE: (recovering a bit, dabbing her eyes) Tish, Laughterobics is so simple you won't believe people haven't thought of it before!

TISH: Tell me about it!

NURLENE: Laughter-obics. Laughter-obics. What does the word tell you?

TISH: (furrowed brow) Well . . . I'm hearing the word "laughter." And I'm hearing "aerobics." Laughterobics! You don't mean laughing is a kind of way of doing aerobics!

NURLENE: (laughing again, air whistling through her triumphantly) Tish, that's *exactly* what I mean! We can actually *stimulate* ourselves through laughter. We can actually *get our heart rate up* through laughter. We can actually *improve our health, alleviate our stress,* and *feel better about ourselves* through laughter!

TISH: (shaking her head) Gosh, Nurlene—I can't imagine that those aren't benefits that would be welcomed by a lot of *these people here* . . .

At this point, with one chunky but expert white wrist, Tish suddenly swept out her arm to include the Network Breakfastees.

Where once they had just been an unthinking, unseeing, unhearing fourth wall, apparently now the audience was subtly being invited into the world of Laughterobics. Bronwyn looked at the group out of the corner of one eye. Smiles were pasted on their faces like masks.

What eventually came out was that Tish and Nurlene would be your hosts for a special Laughterobics cruise that was taking off to Puerto Vallarta the following month.

"Are there still seats available?" Tish asked, opening her eyes worriedly, wonderingly.

"You know . . ." Nurlene leaned forward confidingly. "There are just a few. Just a few. But they're going fast. You should sign up A . . . S . . . A . . . P to guarantee your seat, ya know what I mean?" On this last "ya know what I mean?" Nurlene waggled her fingers around an imaginary cigar in a brisk imitation of Groucho Marx.

The reference was recognized. A brave laugh from the group was procured.

"Ya see?" Nurlene persisted, ostensibly to Tish but really to the rest. "I knew this crowd would loosen up! They're feeling that stress leaving them already! Nothin' wrong with this group that a little laughter won't take care of!"

Just one low price of $3,400 bought you top deck bunking and five days of fun on the *Princess Vallarta*. (A color poster of the boat was set up on an easel, which Tish whipped out for the purpose. At the bottom of the poster, a white square of paper which read: "Laughterobics! With Tish and Nurlene," had been pasted, obscuring whatever had been there before.) Every day, Tish and Nurlene promised to lead two Laughterobics sessions, one in the morning and one in the evening.

By the end of the cruise, participants would be tanned, rested, and most important, would have laughed all their problems away.

"I should know," Nurlene broke in, suddenly somber. "Breast cancer! That was me."

The group of Networking Breakfastees looked faintly terrified. Shoulders in dark gray suits edged forward.

"That's right." She nodded her head, admitting the worst. "Five years ago I was diagnosed. Worst day of my life."

"How did you get through it?" Tish breathed, eyes brimming with tears.

"Chemotherapy . . ." Nurlene replied. Then jabbed Tish in the side for the punch line. "And *laughter*! I just *laughed* that cancer away! And today I'm fit as a fiddle and ready to rock and roll!"

"My mother!" Tish announced to the group. "Isn't she wonderful!"

The Networking Breakfastees broke into spontaneous applause, finally won over, some rising from their seats.

"See you in Puerto Vallarta!" Nurlene hollered, waving her large fleshy arm.

As soon as the meeting was over . . .

Bronwyn slipped down to the underground garage, trying to keep her steps calm and even. Sanitary and attractive. Sanitary and attractive. She clacked past the parking stalls, cradling their sleek BMWs, Audis, Volvos. The occasional Toyota Supra, Honda Prelude, or Acura Integra was always spanking new and definitely LX, with leather interiors.

There was nary a single "Trojans!" bumper sticker anywhere, no sign of humanity at all. No: almost every vehicle looked newly detailed, as sleek and anonymous as a rental.

Which brought her to their own parking slot.

All right. She had to be realistic. The Geo *was* a bit smaller than the others. The interior was black vinyl, not leather.

On the other hand, there was a spoiler and a sunroof. Never mind that the sunroof had started to stick a bit—the others would have no way of knowing that.

The point was, the basic archetype of an expensive sports car was there. Plus the Geo was shiny, brand-new, and electric-blue. They had paid top dollar, driven it straight off the lot. Surely they would be forgiven. She and Paul were a perky young couple after all. Full of potential. All the right instincts. In two or three years, they too would be Volvo-bound.

They were not to blame. They were not to blame—

She stooped to look underneath.

Sure enough, there it was. A venomous, spreading puddle of oil. SANITARY and ATTRACTIVE. Oh my God.

Underneath that brave blue exterior, the Geo was dying inside, hemorrhaging, its lifeblood seeping out.

Bronwyn suddenly had the idea that their old car, the battered white VW bus, had cursed it, had thrown it one last baleful evil eye while the orange-jumpsuited men of Skip Miller Chevy/Geo were dragging it away. Certainly something was always a bit wrong with the Geo, what with its faulty blinker and the sunroof and now this oil thing . . .

But she had to focus now. Bronwyn put her hand over her chest to calm herself. Clean it up. Clean it up. Now. Before anyone else saw. Or at least sop up the bulk of it before they had a chance to get some of that Builder's Emporium stuff. Which would involve driving the car away, revealing the Oil Spots, naked.

But she needed help.

Paul, off with Henry, wouldn't be home for hours.

And then she thought: The maid. The maid was coming today. In—Bronwyn looked at her watch—twenty minutes. Concepción could help her. Good. Small problem, easily handled. Twenty minutes was plenty of time to finish cleaning up the condo. Which she always made sure to do before the maid came. After all, she didn't want Concepción to think that she and Paul lived like pigs.

Back in the apartment, whistling with determined purpose and cheer, Bronwyn rebagged the trash, wiped the cutting board, put CDs back in sleeves. She removed the stacks of bills from their lone piece of furniture, their new washed-pine dining table ($475 at Conran's Habitat, on the Visa), sponged down the kitchen counters, even swabbed out the toilet bowl.

Okay! Okay! It was nine thirty-one. Concepción would be walking in at any moment. And things looked . . . fine. Perfectly fine.

Brownyn settled herself neatly into the lone easy chair they'd dragged from Tujunga and picked up an issue of *Redbook,* immersing herself in its pages. She did not ordinarily read *Redbook,* but she'd lifted a copy from the waiting room at Hanelle Sherwood Films because it had a section on twigs. Everyone nowadays was making baskets and things with twigs, and she thought perhaps she should too.

Anyway, it was either *Redbook* or *The New Yorker.* And Bronwyn did not want to be seen by Concepción reading *The New Yorker.* It seemed rather haughty to be reading *The New Yorker* while an underpaid fortyish woman from Mexico swabbed one's floors.

It was a terrible situation anyway to have an underpaid fortyish woman from Mexico swabbing one's floors.

But at least Bronwyn's reading *Redbook* put them more on the same level.

After all, there was no reason Concepción might not idly flip through *Redbook* on her weekends as well. Surely she too had a home and a husband and therefore an interest in varying her menus cheaply and with less fat but without sacrificing great flavor. Oh my God—I'm babbling, Bronwyn thought, as she continued to page through a section on roasts.

But why was Concepción not here? Bronwyn looked at her watch. Nine forty-five. Already. She was supposed to be here fifteen minutes ago.

And then another worry crossed Bronwyn's mind.

Maybe Concepción—with her gray-streaked black hair, her patient wide face, her white uniform and her plastic gloves—had been silently horrified by their filth (which Bronwyn figured must have been the lipsticks she'd left out on the bathroom counter, or possibly there had been some strands of brown hair left in Paul's comb). So much so that . . .

Or maybe it was their lack of furniture. It was true. Except for the washed-pine dining room table and their lone Tujunga chair, they had none. Bronwyn and Paul really had little to sit on except the pearl-gray Berber carpet. The couch and love seat they had ordered were two weeks late. Bronwyn had called and called, but to no avail. Were they lost? What was going on?

Not to mention that they were eating take-out food every night because of a mysterious problem with the gas line, a problem that was supposed to have been fixed last Monday . . .

The point being that no one else at Symphony Towers knew of

Bronwyn and Paul's problems ... except Concepción—mute, enigmatic, quietly Windexing. She saw straight into everyone's insides. She saw exactly how many plates, stereo systems, couches, night tables they had. She saw what magazines people were reading, the books on their shelves. She saw the price tags on the wine, what was in their medicine cabinets—

Concepción saw ... how Bronwyn and Paul were lacking. How Bronwyn and Paul were *not* the same as the others.

And so maybe ... Bronwyn knew it sounded paranoid, but maybe Concepción *wasn't coming back.*

As soon as she formed the thought, she felt a definite tightening in the throat.

Possibly Concepción had even notified the Condo Association, informing them of a problem. No doubt a new pink memo would be slid under the door at any moment ...

"Oh my God," Bronwyn whispered, as she stood on the Berber-carpeted deck of her ocean liner and gazed upon the enormous black glass prisms—Sumitomo, Toshiba—beyond. She felt like some kind of rotten Captain Ahab of a ship upon which something had died. "Have we been rejected by our maid?"

She heard a key in the door.

"Hello? Cleaning?"

Could it be possible? Yes?

If it was, Bronwyn would do anything to ... to clear their reputation with this person.

"Concepción!" she burst forth, in an exclamation of joy, moving swiftly toward the door.

And there she stood, that vision of forgiveness in white blouse and white pants. She was just now pulling up her pink plastic gloves. Concepción, the kindly, the brave, the good soul who, like some extraordinarily rare and charitable guard in a war camp, had not sold Bronwyn and Paul out to the Condo Association. Concepción lifted her gray-streaked head to look at Bronwyn, with an expression of something like alarm.

"Concepción!" Bronwyn cried out, laughing and feeling foolish. "I thought—I thought you weren't coming!"

"Wednesday," Concepción replied, looking about her a bit nervously. "Wednesday I come at ten A.M. Not nine-thirty. Ten."

The schedule! Of course!

This was the way it alternated. It was all coming back to her.

"I—I'm so glad to see you!" Bronwyn could not stop herself from saying. "You look . . . wonderful. What a great bracelet!"

Concepción lifted her wrist in confusion. "Oh . . . oh yes." She nodded, looking a bit dazed.

Bronwyn found herself grasping that wrist, that lovely brown wrist with its tiny gold bracelet, the wrist that flexed Windex bottles and wrinkled as it scrubbed tile, the wrist that had not rung the doorbell of Chris, the Condo Association president, in order to deliver her very well grounded complaints about Paul and Bronwyn's unsatisfactoriness as tenants.

"Can I . . . Can I get you a soda? Something to drink? We don't have much—we've just moved in, you know." Bronwyn moved toward the kitchen. "Which is why all our furniture is not quite here yet. You know how it is with moving companies . . ."

Concepción looked at her for a moment, then bent down to uncoil the power cord of the vacuum. No, of course she did not know how it was with moving companies. Concepción's family probably moved all their own stuff.

"Well anyway," Bronwyn corrected herself, reaching into the almost empty Sub-Zero refrigerator, "here's a Diet Coke. Or do you not want Diet?" Stop, Bronwyn, she thought. Stop. Think. Focus. "I mean—I just assume all women want Diet, which is not to say that you're . . ."

Concepción was. Overweight, that is. But perhaps she was not so given the particular experiences, perspectives, and backgrounds of her culture. Diversity 2000. Diversity 2000. The Latino culture was probably a bit more forgiving—more *reasonable,* really—about things like how much women were supposed to weigh. It was ridiculous, really, this American system that insisted upon . . .

Bronwyn put her fingers to her temples. They were throbbing.

"Diet Coke is okay," Concepción allowed, as she plugged the vacuum in. "Thank you, Mrs. Bronwyn."

Bronwyn gave her the can. Concepción accepted it, nodded.

"Diet Coke is okay." Bronwyn breathed out, feeling her shoulders slump forward in relief. "Diet Coke is okay."

"Ma'am!" a male voice called out from the open door. "We're here to deliver a couch?"

It was here. Finally. Furniture. Thank God!

"Terrific!" Bronwyn sang out, dancing to the door. "Right in here! Bring in our *furniture!*" she called out loudly into the hall, for all to hear.

party central

Bronwyn and Paul decided to go with soul food for their house-warming party.

Actually, it was Bronwyn who decided to go with Petra King's recommendation for the caterer who used a place called Aunt Louise's Kitchen that had just been recognized as a Top Ten Restaurant Pick by *LA LA* magazine.

Paul had gulped a little at the price—$30 a person, putting the price of the food in the $800 to $1,000 range. It felt like a lot to Bronwyn too. But one thing she did know was that they could not get away with hurling a Trader Joe's cheese log and blue-corn tortilla chips out there and devil take the hindmost anymore. Petra King was coming and Colin Martin and all of his people and also the Zibby Tanaka crowd, as well as a select group of Symphony Tower dwellers. They were social contacts and business contacts and Paul could not be humiliated. Not anymore.

The truth was, in this brave new world, Bronwyn had no idea what people were supposed to eat or how they were supposed to eat it or on what kinds of little napkins. That was why you were supposed to hire professional help to make all the decisions. And so then if the food flopped, you could always draw people back into the kitchen and hiss: "I've had it with Rodolphe! I'll never hire him again! Not at those prices!"

And thus purchase yourself a second chance. She supposed.

Anyway, what was $1,000 when they owed the bank $200,000 already? They could even roll the $1,000 into the loan as well, making their mortgage . . . what? An extra three cents a month? It was practically free. Practically.

Bronwyn could tell Paul was not happy, but the fact was, he didn't really know what kinds of refreshments to throw out on a table either. The last party he'd put together himself was as an undergraduate in college. A "kegger." Paul's ancient concept of party snacks was M&M's and pretzels and onion dip. Typical guests were history majors in bike pants and smelly sweat socks.

So Paul had no choice but to hand Bronwyn all the domestic reins on blind faith.

And thus, a new mode of communication started to happen between them. While Bronwyn and Paul did not know if anything they were doing was right, then again they did not know for sure it was wrong.

So they did not argue. They did not verbally disagree. There wasn't enough information.

On the contrary, they spoke ever more carefully to one another. It was as if they were gingerly trying not to crack this new, fragile egglike thing that was their highly leveraged life together. That certain burnished, hopefully sailing-upward tone that they had formerly reserved for talking to Paul's parents now intruded into their voices when they spoke, even in private, to each other.

Not that they weren't having a chance to practice this rhetorical tactic on Dorothy and Hub at every opportunity. "Yes, Dad!" Paul would say on the phone. "The situation at Symphony Towers is strong, strong, strong! Five new units were snapped up today! Because it's downtown, Dad—the middle of the city!"

But now it was pretty much always the way they hailed each other at the end of the day, much like country squires might heartily do when returning from the administration of distant plots of dubious land.

"No problem with the Futura today!" Bronwyn would call out stoutly to Paul, as she set grocery bags on the kitchen counter. "Everything was cool. I think I was just imagining that rattle the other day."

"The disposal is working like a dream!" he'd chime back, in modulations as smooth and sunny as the Waltons'. "Something was just stuck down in there. Got it out with a chopstick. No problem!"

"Terrific!" she'd reply.

And of course, now that their $500-a-night caterer was here, setting up for the evening's housewarming party, they were doing it more than ever. Standing together side by side, they pronounced bits of the new, unaccustomed vocabulary in oddly hearty voices—the voices of strangers, of Pod People.

"This looks like it's going to be wonderful!" Paul said, rubbing the small of her back.

"It does, doesn't it?" she replied automatically, putting her arm around him.

"Good choice on the caterer!"

"I thought about it a lot. It was this or Celine's on Melrose."

"I'm so glad we get to eat hearty food, not just sushi or something too light."

"I think people like to get a nice plate of food at a party, don't you?"

"*I* certainly like to."

Gary the caterer had brought two of his own white china vases to give the table a nice design. He insisted on florals, something perfect for spring: marigolds, a touch of begonia, hydrangea, chrysanthemum—most of them blooms she could neither identify nor spell.

"I want to set you up with a beautiful table, a really beautiful table," Gary insisted. "I really like to use silverware with a chevron pattern this time of the year, to help us transition into the new season. You did enjoy Chaz, didn't you?"

Bronwyn had. Chaz the stylist had also been recommended by Petra King. And so Bronwyn had obediently gone to a salon where people—staff—flowed over you, people who kept up with fashion magazines, who gossiped in hair salons, who gave you little neck massages, who were into aromatherapy, who plucked their eyebrows—and yours. Indeed. "Your eyebrows are kind of a mess," she had been told at Chaz's. Her eyebrows? A mess? Who knew?

"I'm going to take a shower," Paul said, squeezing her hand.

"All right, sweetie," she replied, squeezing it back.

And yet, even as Bronwyn watched Gary the caterer's eyes and hands fluttering and flowing over everything, pushing the perfectly aged wooden tables together for the party buffet, unstacking the earthenware dishes, scattering dried flowers and twigs everywhere, she felt a pang of regret. She knew now that her little Trader Joe's Boho parties of the past had been awful, cliché, everything wrong. And yet, it had been kind of fun to do it herself, throw a scarf here, some extra tea candles there.

Now she would not even dare touch a basket for fear of doing something wrong, wrecking the shape, lending the wrong . . . *emphasis* or something.

Too bad too about Jonathan.

At the last moment, in a completely unbidden wave of nostalgia, she had tried to telephone him. She knew he was wrong for this group, with his fright wig and his glasses and his sniffing of his long nervous fingers, but . . . A little distance between all of them, and in an odd way Bronwyn found that she actually missed her and Jonathan's awful Gallo chartreuse sunset conversations in that ratty old Tujunga house.

But the phone number at Jonathan's new place was disconnected, or perhaps just wrong. And so they had received no word back from him. He was probably busy with his new computer company.

Either way, it all gave Bronwyn a sad, forlorn feeling.

"Oh . . . my . . . God!"

Petra King. It was she. She stood at Bronwyn and Paul's front door, arms raised to the heavens in a kind of salute, clad like one of the pilgrims in Chaucer's *Canterbury Tales*.

On Petra King the outfit worked—indeed it was almost as though she held herself beautifully still, that extra second, to give her audience that moment to contemplate it. The floppy black velvet cloche hat with rhinestone pin large as a boil, the oversized silk taupe Dolce & Gabbana dress shirt which fluttered down over her knees, the hilariously long—but outrageously expensive— chains of pearls and gems and schmook, the tiny little olive-green lace-up boots from Maud Frizon, $600.

A heavier-hipped woman might have ballooned in such an outfit. But Petra King weighed 107. She could wear a muumuu and you'd still see those papery cheekbones, the fine slivers of tendons in her neck, the birdlike breastbones. Each long vertical fold in her whispering silk—conspicuously more folds than other women would have, as though it were a stick puppet that lived inside the caftan, not a woman—spoke of yet another Mrs. Fields pumpkin–walnut–chocolate chip muffin left untasted.

Petra King did not venture east of Laurel Canyon often, as everyone knew. And yet she was here, for a mere housewarming party, at Bronwyn and Paul's. It was a triumph.

A triumph fraught with anxiety, however. What payment might she exact for this magnanimous gesture? Bronwyn braced herself for the attack. When would her laser-beam eyes dart the wrong way? "This ficus is *not well*," she had heard Petra say once, fingering a wilted leaf in ill-masked repulsion.

Regardless, Petra King was here now, her thin birdlike manicured hand clutching a $50 bottle of Gold Label Krug vintage 1986 champagne swathed gently in slender silver ribbons, upping the gift ante yet again.

And so Bronwyn would stand tall. She had hired the professional help recommended. They could not be blamed. Paul could not be excluded from the world of television and film based merely on that.

"I love it," Petra declared grandly, easy and generous with her love today, willing to dispense it to the right and to the left in loose $5 and $10 denominations.

She stepped forward into Bronwyn and Paul's brand-new marble mini-foyer and did a slow twirl, causing her shirt dress to gently rise around her, then to fall again.

It suddenly occurred to Bronwyn that there was no discernible style to the Symphony Towers condo. The track lighting, the pine sideboards, the faux granite in the bathroom. Was this Danish Modern? Zen Garden? Contemporary American? Whatever it was, recently the whole place had started to strike Bronwyn as just . . . a bit harsh.

Not Petra.

She took Bronwyn's sweaty hands in her own.

"I love it," Petra repeated simply, dramatic in her surrender. "The high ceilings, the air, the light. This is home," she murmured softly, as though in possession of some deep spiritual insight. "This is home."

"These are our neighbors Fred and Lita," Bronwyn put in, determinedly. Fred and Lita looked perfect this evening, dressed in beige, tortoiseshell rims, blank faces.

"Petra King," Petra said, glancing them over appraisingly.

"Fred is in advertising," Bronwyn blundered on. "And Lita here—Lita is a graphic—"

"The busy screenwriter!" Petra segued smoothly, shifting her attention as Paul appeared in the hallway. Fred and Lita looked blank for a moment, then shuffled off to the food table, their duties clearly done. Petra indicated the foyer again, breathless, shaking her cloche hat for emphasis. "This is sensational! I love it!"

Fortunately, Petra's timing was perfect: the bulk of the party—Colin Martin, Henry Marcus, the rest of them—already stood in the long white glassed-in living room, drinking champagne, the buzz already launched and whizzing.

"Harold sends his regrets," Petra explained, holding herself still for another moment so that Paul could take her red silk muffler from her to go hang it up. "With the new Ron Howard project, his schedule has been impossible. There's a lot of complicated under-scoring, tons of montage, extra licensing needed what with the bla bla bla bla bla bla—"

"How was the drive?" Bronwyn cut in with the customary humility, to get it over with. "It wasn't too bad, was it?"

A silence hung in the air.

How bad had it been? Had it been an easy fifteen minutes? A horrendous fifty-five? How heroic Petra's efforts were—in any case—to leave Santa Monica, Harold, Natalie, the deck, the stu-dio, Spielberg, their fabulous life to come east and mingle among mere mortals, in a dismal world where she might have to bestir herself from a lovely reverie and actually stop and get gas.

Too, since Petra had actually made the drive to Bronwyn and Paul's *home*—a location they had picked—they would have to bear the brunt of the blame if, God forbid, Petra had had a particularly bad or dangerous drive over.

If the drive downtown was that impossible, well, this might be the last they'd ever see of Petra. Or the already elusive Harold. If Petra decided the thirty-five-minute drive was too much to be borne by ordinary humans, buying a place down here could be seen as a very bad move for Bronwyn and Paul. It could be fatal, a humiliation.

"Not bad," Petra replied with a touching bravery, once again squeezing the sack of her charity and allowing a few droplets to sprinkle out. Bronwyn held herself very still: Petra was being very sweet, but was this all?

Petra's brow then furrowed slightly—but without wrinkling. It was a weird effect that gave her skin the look of some sort of fairly lifelike latex.

"Even though I realize in hindsight I should have stayed on the

101 to Temple, rather than heading west on the 10. Got a *little* turned around!" Petra continued humorously, indulging finally in a big guffaw, letting it titter out of her. Faces were gradually turning toward her, bobbing on her every word.

"And suddenly I think I was in Little Tokyo! Had I been driving *that* long? Maybe I should have packed a sandwich! I love this view!" Petra changed tactics suddenly—just when things were getting dicey—moving forward to the line of windows. They were steel frames of rectangular glass that cracked open a breezy but— in deference to the condo's elevation—safe six inches. Through them, chrome-and-glass skyscrapers were visible, done in their hues of black, granite, onyx. Far below was the ribbon of Figueroa Boulevard upon which traffic crawled.

"I absolutely love it! I'm thrilled to be down here," she assured Bronwyn, touching her wrist. "I love the energy of downtown!" A muffled crash tingled from street level. Petra raised her eyebrows and peered out the window. "Looks like you have great security too," she continued, with a studied blandness.

"Terrific security," Paul rushed in. "The best. There are guards in the lobby and in the garage on call twenty-four hours a day."

"It's actually very safe," Bronwyn chimed in, "because we *are* so careful. And besides, more and more people are moving down here—there's a real influx that's turning the neighborhoods around. It's not just offices down here, it's turning into a real bedroom community."

"There are a thousand new condo units on this block alone," Paul pointed out.

"We can practically walk to the Music Center, to MOCA—"

"And we're five minutes away from the best sushi in town—"

"It's great to live in a real city! It's like New York!"

"I leave the studio—and I'm home in ten minutes! It's cut my commute down by forty-five minutes! That's an extra hour and a half a day!"

"There's a whole new renaissance going on in downtown!" Bronwyn finished. "Every day is exciting. A lot of other buyers are trying to get into this building. We're too happy!"

Bronwyn pushed open the door to the buffet . . .

Which was perfect.

The dinner would prove to be the high point of Bronwyn's thirtieth year, the climax, the impossible dream—the sense of rightness, of control of her surroundings, and therefore of home—fully realized. In the cataclysmic months that followed, she would remember each detail, each aroma, each fleck of caraway pepper, each mini-rib in spicy special Palagro sauce, the exotic greens tossed ever so lightly in vinegar, the buttery rolls so rough on the outside and yet fluffy as clouds on the inside, the hand-painted earthenware platters so handsome and yet satisfyingly rustic, cloth napkins in rust and dark olive, wine glasses balloon-bowled and yet thin-stemmed.

Gary the caterer, clad understatedly in yellow cashmere turtleneck and starched white apron, a mini log cabin pinned to his maroon tweed vest, supervised as Bronwyn and Paul carried the generous glazed bowls of garlic mashed potatoes and ginger coleslaw out from her perfect kitchen . . .

Her perfect kitchen, with its cool white Sub-Zero refrigerator with tempered glass no-spill shelves, its Corian backsplash, its Kohler sink, its recessed lighting, its bleached pine paneling. The kitchen to end all kitchens.

The conversation of her good-looking guests, their hair cut beautifully, the swish of their beautiful fabrics, the mascara lightly brushed on eyelashes, the pleasing soft flush of MAC's more exclusive lip colors. Bronwyn loved it all.

Because there was Paul, her Paul, in the middle—handsome, tall, with the new, more flattering and somber wire-frames, in his new linen jacket, talking with people, them wanting to talk to him, relaxed on his own turf, in his own lair, in his own kingdom. Here, at their luxurious clean-lined condo, at the center of downtown, at the cultural center of L.A., an exciting burgeoning nineties city.

And what were these exciting people talking about, here at the hub of the civilized world? Bronwyn moved closer in, as though she were a camera dollying in on a marvelous scene in a movie.

"Did you hear the NPR piece on the Columbus Quincentennial?" Henry was saying. Bronwyn hadn't of course, she hadn't listened to the radio or read the paper ever since the night she snapped off NPR in the Geo. "Now some people want to call it 'Indigenous Peoples' Day, to commemorate the Indians. They want to get rid of Christopher Columbus memorials altogether. In Oregon, they actually want to take his statue down. I for one am offended!"

"Offended!" There was a titter.

"Oh come on," JC Curtis, an *L.A. Weekly* theater reviewer, was saying flatly, pulling at her cigarette. "There has been so much victimization of minorities in this country, it's old news. Columbus is *tired,* man. Eurocentrism is tired. It's a fait accompli. It's done. They should have gotten rid of Columbus Day a long time ago."

Henry was getting excited. His cheeks flushed. He clearly thrived on this.

"What about me? I'm an American, born in this country. My own ancestors were Italian! From the Old Country. As a matter of fact, there were a few shipbuilders and navigators amongst them. This is my heritage too—"

"A heritage of enslavement, opportunism, capitalism, and murder," JC fired back. "If that's what makes an 'American' heritage, count me out! I want no part of it—"

"You want enslavement, let's talk about the Jews!" Henry retorted. "Italian Jews! The fifteenth century was a terrible time for Italian Jews! We were working as indentured servants in farms held by the Medicis! The Catholic church was all over us like a coat!"

"Oh come on! That was five centuries ago!"

"And slavery in America is new news? The African-Americans—I don't even know why we use that term, are we Americans or not?—keep harping back to that—"

"You are such a sick white male disgusting—"

"Male-bashing! Sure, go ahead and male-bash me! It's the fashionable thing to do, isn't—"

"Especially when all this Rodney King stuff is going on. I can't believe you—"

The white searchlights of a helicopter swept across the living room, like klieg lights searching for A-list guests.

At first Bronwyn thought nothing of it.

Occasionally helicopters did wheel about in the sky—this was L.A., and they were so high up—so she and Paul had not thought much of it these past few weeks when they were getting ensconced in the Towers. If anything, helicopters wheeling was a good sign—

it meant the police were out and patrolling, just doing their rounds, making sure everything was in place.

By the third time the big choppers swung by, their searchlights bouncing agitatedly like some laser show, a few people turned slightly and looked over their shoulders.

"God, they're really out tonight," remarked Henry. "They're looking for *somebody*."

"What's going *on*?" murmured another guest.

"Has anyone checked into the verdicts recently?" Nancy the actress said suddenly.

"Oh, that won't be settled for days . . ."

Verdicts? An image floated to Bronwyn of some fuzzy video-taped thing—bad lighting, a parked car, the jagged motions of cops agitatedly moving over a blobby shape. But she had flipped past the news, flipped past it, all of it being too much for her now.

At that moment, slowly, inevitably, they heard the sound of a fire engine siren rising from the distance.

Bronwyn could not intellectually grasp the possible implications, but an ominous feeling was coming over her. She had the sense of something moving out there, something massive, something that had to do with that blobby murky shape, something that had its own momentum completely outside of her, something that might trample her in its path, not a personal thing, but a violent natural force, something vaguely bad for the Towers.

Everyone held themselves still and silent.

There was another faint crash from far, far below, muted through the tempered-glass window. It was a clanking, a kind of metal-on-metal sound, sort of like a trash can being hurled.

And there they stood, in their glass-enclosed tower, on the

twenty-seventh floor. Another helicopter made a pass at the window next to the kitchen, urgently, like a bird beating its wings at a cage.

In one quick swoop, like God's hand lightly wafting over the scene, the triangular Art Deco wall sconces went out.

In one sickening lurch, all moved quickly to the windows. There was no need for speech. Speech had become irrelevant at this point.

When Bronywn looked down, she dearly wanted to see the pristine granite-and-glass faces of skyscrapers, the slowly moving traffic on the clean boulevard, the little dwarf trees in their little dwarf pots. When she looked down, she wanted to will downtown into its customary sleekness, smoothness.

But it was clear that something was wrong.

At the foot of the building, agitating the landscape, flashed the red and blue lights—almost Christmassy—of three police cars.

Bronwyn felt the usual clench of fear when she saw those flashing red and blue lights. Those lights were always the bringers of bad news. "Please step away from your vehicle, ma'am. May I see your license and registration, please?" Flashlights would be poked in one's face, grim pronouncements given. Or they meant someone's window had been broken, the sanctity of the home violated, TV sets rudely wrested from the inside of the house, entrails of wires and things hanging, like a bad cesarean.

Sometimes, as one knew from prime-time TV, a twisted body would be pulled out on a stretcher, you'd hear the harsh crackle of police radios, the doors of a house would stand all open, unnaturally bright lights blazing out into the night, someone's wife in a blue denim shirt, her blond hair in a ponytail, would sit at her kitchen table weeping with a red face.

But no.

These three police cars sat one in front of the other, politely hushed, orderly. Their lights flashed, flashed, flashed, but they seemed oddly disconnected. The cars weren't going anywhere. No tickets were being issued, no arrests were being made. They were simply waiting. For what?

Bronwyn's gaze shifted, and the answer became clearer.

To their right, up Third Street, there was a dark twisted knot, like a parked car, but with an odd shape to it. Swarming around it like fruit flies was a small, excited, disorganized crowd who appeared to be bashing at the car with clubs and boards. They would spin and dance, then bash again, as though part of an eerie Walpurgis Night ritual.

Flickering at the car's front hood was the tiny, gold, evil eye of flames. Black smoke unfurled above like a funnel reaching up, reaching up to pollute the air around the skyscrapers.

As the horrified guests watched, more fruit fly–size revelers began to stream in from two directions, from Third, from the west on Figueroa. It was like a parade. But without the stately order of, say, the Rose Parade, with its pastel Anheuser-Busch and Kraft Cheez Whiz floats from which lightly narcotized Pasadena High School teen girls waved white gloves.

This parade was propelled forward with its own energy, excitement, urgency. Its members moved in the rhythm of discovery, two or three particles streaming forward in three different directions, pieces of the group following each, sometimes not following, sometimes glomming backwards to attach themselves onto a tree, a car, a telephone booth, a bus bench. It was like an amoeba convulsed with the asexual ecstasy of separating and dividing itself, of multiplying itself over the earth, the sea, the concrete.

The streaming, dividing organism was bashing the terrain with clubs as it moved forward. Now the distant crashing sound was a reality, familiar, arrhythmic, a part of the sonic blanket.

And now little fireballs were flying out of the pulsing, disorganized army. Yes. They were. Glittering yellow balls, little tiny eyes grafted from the large evil eye in the car, stroked across the air, some falling fallow, some bursting into little bouquets of flame, becoming evil eyes of their own.

But what of the cops? Still they sat, quite, cramped, motionless. The red and blue lights still flashed, but without coherence, without authority. The tide was lapping closer, victoriously, cheerfully. The cops, the tide. The cops, the tide. It was like two elements in a biblical story.

And then, the tide was upon them.

"Oh my God," some nameless female guest said with quavering voice. It didn't matter who, she spoke for all.

The fruit flies were bashing the cop cars viciously, lifting them, shaking them, exulting. One of the red and blue lights went out in a bang, stopped flashing. Still the other two flashed, like last call for the carousel at some kind of carnival, the popcorn stands closing, the parking attendants gathering up sawhorses.

"There goes ... the neighborhood," Henry observed, in an odd, throaty voice, finally finding his tongue.

The intercom chirped. The partyers, huddled in the dark, stirred in either excitement or fear.

Bronwyn was moved by the former.

"Thank God!" she cried out, leaping to her feet. "The police are here!" She had been calling 911, to almost no avail. First there'd been no dial tone. Then 911 emitted a strange busy signal. Finally she'd gotten through—but the dispatcher she reached expressed helplessness, the circuits had been overwhelmed. They'd try to send a car out, which might come, it might not, due to the overflow of calls . . .

Meanwhile, the howling mob down below seemed to have continued up Figueroa, passing them. A certain odd quiet had settled in. Bronwyn was ready for order, a return to normal, a closing of the terrible eye of the hurricane. Paul had gone down with Gary and Fred into the garage to check the circuit breakers.

The chirping intercom was like a call from Order.

"Hello!" she spoke to the intercom. "Hello?"

There was a crackling sound. Static. "Ho!" a distant voice called out. "Hellll—"

"Hello!" Bronwyn tried again. "Police?"

More static.

"Are they coming up?" Nancy the actress called out. "What should we do? Should we try to get out of here? Is it safe to get into our cars?"

"Hello?" Bronwyn persisted. Grimly she said: "I have to go down there to let them in."

"Do you think there's a possibility it's . . . not the cops?" Lita asked.

Bronwyn grabbed a flashlight.

"Do you want someone to go with you?" Henry asked.

"I'll just be a second," she replied, attempting but the shakiest rendition of her and Paul's hearty, hopeful sailing-upward tone. "I'm sure this will all be over within the hour."

"Um, there is cake!" she added. "There is really good pineapple upside-down . . ." Her voice trailed off. What am I saying? she thought.

"Be careful," a chorus of murmurs begged her.

Incredibly, the elevator was working. It seemed that just the fuses powering her floor of condos had blown. Feeling like Bruce Willis in some sort of *Dead Something* action picture, Bronwyn gripped her flashlight.

Part of her brain wanted to descend into hysteria. A small voice was screaming: Symphony Towers . . . is located in a war zone! No one else will ever buy in! Vacancy rates will remain high! The value will drop! We're mortgaged to the hilt! Dead meat! Dead meat! We will lose everything!

She almost imagined that if she'd looked too closely outside her ocean liner windows she'd have seen Paul's parents, Hub and Dorothy, as faint as holograms, bobbing through the swirling black air like in *The Wizard of Oz*. Their old eyes were sad and wide and horrified. Their hands were spread. "Bronwyn," they were mouthing. "We trusted you. For your savvy business sense. Where is our twenty-six thousand dollars? Where is our twenty-six thousand dollars?"

She could imagine in slow motion the old dog-eared bundles of bank statements, rubber-banded together in their plastic bags, tumbling slowly through the ember-filled air. Hub and Dorothy, ghostlike, tried in vain to catch them—the mutual funds, the savings statements, the bank deposits—but it was all falling past them down into the street, down into the mob.

But she would not listen to that voice. She couldn't. She couldn't give over to despair, to the knowledge, now, that everything was wrong. That they had done everything wrong. That they had walked straight into a hall of mirrors.

But no. To give over to it would be to surrender—and how many people were depending on her? It would be the most selfish thing to do, to give over to despair. She couldn't. She couldn't. She must be strong.

"Get a grip," she muttered to herself, "get a grip."

She had to turn this into a heroic rescue mission. She would protect the group if she had to lay her own body down across Figueroa. They were her responsibility, her task, her crusade.

But when she approached the foyer, she could see that it was not the police beyond the glass door.

Slumped against the intercom button was a disheveled, even dirty-looking dark-skinned figure. It was wearing an odd, tattered kind of skirt and, most distressingly, this kind of orange headpiece from which leaves and twigs poked out. There even seemed to be a bit of blood smeared on the left temple.

Bronwyn felt a surge of horror combined equally with nausea and disappointment. It was clearly a lost, crazy homeless person of some kind. It was unfortunate that this person—it looked like an old woman—had been caught in the cross fire. She could see helping this ragged homeless person back upstairs to her kitchen, her gleaming white kitchen.

But what then?

What of the danger? To her and her guests? And what would the Condo Association . . .

She felt a chill. SANITARY and ATTRACTIVE. SANITARY and ATTRACTIVE. This person was neither. Who knew what condo rules she would be breaking?

It's just that my own situation is so tenuous, she wanted to tell the person. I'd love to help you. But I can't. Because Paul and I will lose everything we . . . We'll have to get our own shopping cart, our own rags, begin our own long sad march . . .

Nervously, she approached the glass. The figure, though slumped, was breathing regularly. The ragged orange dress was heaving in and out, in and out. That dress, there was something faintly . . . something faintly Thanksgiving pageant about it. Bronwyn couldn't place it. She had noticed that homeless people sometimes looked like festive if filthy wandering minstrels escaped from some Renaissance *faire* . . .

Colonial American women. For a moment, Bronwyn had the fantasy that what slumped before her was a kind of tired Sarah Kemble Knight, exhausted by her cooking and her poetry, come to haunt her doorstep . . .

But no. This person would be fine for the moment. She would be fine. Beyond, Figueroa now stood completely quiet, empty, piles of trash humped along the sidewalk like laundry. Probably the person was in no immediate danger . . .

Bronwyn could call 911 again. Certainly. The lines were starting to go back to normal. That was the best thing to do for all concerned. That was what the responsible, smart Condo Owner would do, using good thought and judgment.

As she turned, resolute, ready to handle the situation in a socially responsible—not needlessly foolish and dangerous—way she had just a second of trepidation. It was the feeling, it was that same tiny, nagging feeling as when they had taken the old white VW bus away like Old Yeller.

It was just a car, she breathed to herself. Just a car! She turned deliberately back toward the elevator. But as she did so, she somehow felt very close to weeping.

part three

———

abyss

underdogs

Bronwyn lay on her Wamsutta 100% goose-down pillows swathed in 200-thread Percale sheets on her queen-size sleigh bed with a bottle of Stolichnaya and finally got to know her neighborhood . . .

By watching hour after hour of Horrible Riot Scenes.

Or as she called it, "My Riots"—since the riots were about her, of her, and because of her.

There were scenes of poor black and Latino looters—their brown faces stretched into wild grins—as they trundled gaily out of the smashed front window of a store, goods tucked under their arms in a weirdly joyous free-for-all. Some even waved to the camera, as though they were in some terrible *America's Funniest Home Videos* gone awry.

But what were they carrying? Bronwyn leaned forward. Pampers, sponges, bottles of orange juice. The camera panned up to the awning. "$1 and Under."

"Why? Why?" Bronwyn pleaded. "These things only *cost* a dollar! Why didn't they go to the Neiman Marcus shoe department? And get something *worth* stealing!"

Oddly enough, she kind of identified with the idea of going into a store and just grabbing everything off the shelves. Wouldn't she love to go to Conran's Habitat and just fill up her cart? Butcher-block cutting boards, Italian ceramic pots, three-foot-high wrought-iron candlesticks?

But if she'd been televised, everyone would see her and know she had stolen everything. The important thing was not the objects themselves but that you made enough to buy such lovely objects. That was where status came from. That was the point. Wasn't it?

As it was, she and Paul had hurled all their stuff on the Visa. They would be suffering later for the butcher-block cutting boards and Italian ceramicware, like ... honest Americans. Wouldn't they?

The scene shifted to a heavily bearded Latino man, dressed like a construction worker in T-shirt and low-slung jeans, who was laughing as he smashed bottles of milk onto the sidewalk. For no purpose but hate.

"The hate," Bronwyn breathed. "The hate."

There was so much hate on their television. It was a Saturday morning Film Festival of Hate. A more terrifying, fully televised PR reversal for the oppressed minorities of the city could not have been planned. In blazing Technicolor slow motion, there was looting, stumbling, jeering, gesticulating.

In another scene, three fashionably dressed Latino teenagers—who on another night might have been featured discoing with Julie Brown on the laser-lit dance floor of Club MTV—drank beers and laughed as they watched a Korean electronics store burn to the ground. They laughed. The orange of the fire reflected in their sunglasses, in their white teeth, in the bounce of the girl's brazen gold hoop earrings. The hate, the hate.

In another, the camera panned across a panoply of brown and black faces—their eyes glittering and crafty—calculating how best to tie a stolen mattress down onto the roof of a beat-up little blue Hyundai to drag it home to their tiny apartment. Windows were kicked in. Sweating fat women rifled madly through boxes of Reebok athletic shoes. Mean-mouthed teenagers in *Ghostbuster* T-shirts sauntered out of a Thrifty wearing five hats stacked one on top of another.

It was a terrible carnival in which old men and old women and nubile young girls and even children, even children, participated. Entire Guatemalan families were out, their large asses filling the camera as they bent over to gather armfuls of Walkmans, Cabbage Patch dolls, corn cobs, whatever. It was a Brueghel painting come to life, in the most violent way.

A terrible carnival.

The thing with the homeless person had been a mistake, of course.

Bronwyn hadn't been to blame. This person was buzzing her in the middle of a riot, for crying out loud. By opening the door she would have been endangering an entire building. She had done the right thing by immediately dialing 911.

The woman really had looked exactly like a homeless person or a bag lady or something.

There was no way Bronwyn could have known—as she had found out later, in a heart-tugging *L.A. Times* article—that this was a middle-class Asian person. A college graduate. In fact, a Ph.D. candidate—just like she had been—in Ethnic Studies at Cal

State Dominguez Hills. Even worse, a multicultural performance artist, dressed, for a Columbus Quincentennial arts event, in the costume of a Native American.

My God, Bronwyn thought. What has happened to me?

I was throwing a $1,000 soul food party in a white skyscraper called Symphony Towers and barred from my door a performance artist dressed as a Native American during riots for a verdict I didn't even know had happened.

Of the acts of riot-time heroism reported in the papers, Bronwyn would not be one. No. She would fall thoroughly on the coward side. The evil side. The bad side.

But then, things got worse.

While flipping through the channels on the fifth day of her Stolichnaya-induced stupor, Bronwyn found a local cable station that was carrying a live event from a place called the OtherVoices Performance Complex.

It was called "The Beating of Rodney King Performance Festival."

It began with the lighting of candles, commemorating, as an African-American woman with tiny high bun and granny bifocals announced, "a moment of silence to respect . . . to *respect,* the true heroes of April: the L.A. Four." She crossed her arms across her chest.

The L.A. Four. The four guys who had tried to beat Reginald Denny's brains out with a fire extinguisher.

Then came a tall slender Latina with a punk haircut. Salsa music came on. The Latina danced, in this kind of mocking exaggerated way, she lifted small decorative items out of a shiny little pot . . . a pot that looked very much like it had come from the Four Winds Emporium.

Bronwyn leaned forward in horror. Was it—But yes, in a moment of sickening horror, she realized that it was one of the little brass elephant planters . . . exactly one of the ones she had bought so many of on that day of the sale, exactly the one she had given to Colin Martin at his housewarming party.

As the Latina danced, she sang this hideous, taunting song:

> I am not your chatch-ka
> I am not your chatch-ka
> I am not your chatch-ka
> Don't hang me on your door!

All the items she lifted out of the pot were in fact . . . ethnic accessories of the kind Bronwyn had always loved to buy from the Four Winds Emporium. Wind chimes . . . made of dancing sombreros. Wooden salt and pepper shakers . . . carved in the shape of cacti. The batik scarf, just like the one she'd hung on the rearview mirror of the VW.

And finally . . .

She lifted out the last item, but Bronwyn already knew what was coming . . .

The Chicana lifted out a pair of earrings. They were Bronwyn's earrings exactly. The Guatemalan dolls.

"I am not your chatch-ka," the Chicana spat out, crushing one earring in each hand.

So this was the way it was.

Bronwyn's not letting the ethnic person in was not a solitary mistake, committed in the heat of the moment.

No. This ethnic oppression was the road Bronwyn had been

traveling for a long, long time. Subconsciously. Subjugating them. She had reduced people of other colors to a style of decor.

She was to blame.

She had let the world down.

"Don't you see, Paul? We did this. We did this. All of this."

To her amazement, Paul just laughed, morose.

"Please, Bronwyn. Stop believing everything the *L.A. Times* tells you."

"How can you say something like that? Don't you see, Paul? We're white!"

"We are the oppressors! Sure!" he exclaimed.

And so began the terrible fight between them.

He plumped himself down on the edge of the queen-size sleigh bed—the one he had always hated and had been opposed to buying in the first place.

"How are we responsible for the ills of society? Since when were we given that much control? Last time I checked, your Women's Studies program was supplanted by an Ethnic Studies program. Last time I checked, you'd lost your job. Last I checked, it was us the Condo Association was trying to kick out. Last I checked, it looks like I may lose my job too. They don't want white writers on the Diversity 2000 project anymore—"

"But don't you see that the world, this whole world, is run by white men?"

"White men? Like me? Like Jonathan? You mean the guy who's homeless?"

It was true. Jonathan had been sleeping in his car.

It seemed Jonathan had put his half of Hub and Dorothy's $52,000 into Hoffstead Software Systems. Most of his $26,000 had gone into leasing a small office space in North Hollywood, purchasing top-of-the-line computer gear for high-speed number crunching, and even, she'd heard, as much as $9,000 trying to push his patent through (the lawyer fees had been astronomical).

All this only to find that Microsoft had already invented software to do what his did which ran twice as fast. They were giving it away, free, with every Windows purchase. Apparently, they were taking over the software market so completely that if you didn't buy everything Microsoft for your computer, none of it would work together. Buying some clever little gizmo like Jonathan's would be like putting a baboon heart into a baby.

Bronwyn didn't say anything for a moment.

"Last time I checked, the only people we looted were my parents, seventy-year-old people whose families lost their farms way back when, the whitest people in the world. With the new plunge in real estate prices, they're about to lose their savings again."

Paul slumped forward, a silhouette of despair against the fading light.

"You know who identifies with Rodney King?" he whispered. "I do. I feel totally down and beaten, and still the world keeps coming back and beating me and beating me and beating me."

Those were the most horrible words Bronwyn had ever heard spoken. And by Paul, her Paul. She closed her eyes and put her hands over her ears.

It was later that night, TV still going on in the back, that Bronwyn appeared to Paul in a nightgown, like an wraith.

She was mumbling brokenly.

"In preriot days, it was enough to listen to NPR and remember birthdays and ask after people's health and support them in their careers and to refer them to helpful bits in the *Times* and read good selections from the Quality Paperback Club and try not to mix too many different alcohols together in one evening so you didn't throw up later. You recycled, you sent fifteen dollars to the Children's Mission, you gave all your old clothes to the Salvation Army.

"You know, your neighborhood was given to you, it was given to you, and you functioned as best you could, within the rules of that neighborhood.

"You didn't have to be held accountable for the . . . the *demographic composition* of that neighborhood. No—you were one of many peons, struggling to do your best. Nowadays, look what's expected from a decent person. You have to be an expert on . . . on everything!"

She waved the *L.A. Times* forlornly at him. A meaningless stream of jumbled statistics spewed out of her.

"I never knew about the fifty-three percent unemployment for adult black males and how welfare checks only amount to seven hundred and thirty-seven dollars a month and how a quart of milk costs a dollar eighty-nine in the inner city and about sickle cell anemia and the fall in blue-collar machinist jobs due to the toppling infrastructure of Southern California aerospace and the Latinization of Boyle Heights and the new black-brown conflict and how in the last five years the choke hold and the half nelson have been outlawed or not outlawed by Daryl Gates.

"What do they expect of me? No, no—not 'they.' There is no 'they.' 'They' is 'us.' What do us expect of me? Or is 'me' actually 'them'? What do us expect of 'them'? Is this even grammatical? Help!"

Paul could only stare at her as if she were a madwoman.

"The choke hold! The choke hold!" she pushed on. "Why did I not know about the choke hold? This Rodney King thing."

"Noni, it's terrible about the police and what they do . . . but how in God's name can this be your fault? You're not a cop."

He put his arms around her.

"You're not a cop, sweetie. You're not a cop."

"I am," she whispered. "I am."

"I mean, Watts is as much your stomping ground as—as Beverly Hills. Maybe you don't know about the choke hold, but sweetie, you don't know anything about high finance either. We're just kind of . . . in the middle. Lost."

"You let one thing slip and suddenly there's a riot. And that's what I did. I turned off NPR. I turned off NPR. I put on the Wave."

"It's all right, sweetie. It's all right. Don't blame yourself. Blame Kenny G."

"All I wanted was a kitchen."

"A kitchen?" he asked.

And then it came out of her, all in a flow.

"I just wanted a kitchen. Okay, a New England kitchen. But just because I like the blue and the white and the little flowers. A little herb garden in the garden window. Wooden spoons. Not an all-white kitchen. Not an Aryan kitchen. Just a kitchen. I didn't even need the Sub-Zero refrigerator. I just wanted a clean, new refrigerator without grody icebergs in it. A five-hundred-dollar Sears refrigerator would have been fine. Almond color a plus.

"I didn't want a mammy in the kitchen. A big black mammy making pancakes. A slave. No. I wanted to humbly do my own cooking in my own kitchen, on nice pans. On environmentally friendly pans. We would have had a nice bin for recycling. I didn't want to cook veal in my kitchen. Or anything mean. Anything politically awful. Just ... eggplant. Cheese. Coriander. Is that okay? Something with a nice smell. Garlic. Lemon.

"Was that too much to ask? I just wanted a kitchen for you, me, and perhaps a handful of friends. Eventually, perhaps two children of our own.

"But is that wrong? Is it wrong to want a kitchen like that? A kitchen I wallpapered myself?

"By not including a lot of homeless people in my kitchen and angry disenfranchised gang teens, am I somehow excluding them? Should I include them in my kitchen? Should I be cooking for all of them in my kitchen?

"Should my share be a utility closet in my own kitchen? Is it wrong to just want us in our kitchen? I mean, I would have been happy to give up my own job, send checks, volunteer to cook five hours a day in the kitchens of others.

"I just wanted to come home to my own kitchen at the end of the day. But I think it was wrong. I think it was wrong." Her voice dropped to a ragged whisper. "Who was I . . . to think I deserved my own kitchen?"

panorama city

Since it was her riot and her fault, Bronwyn took it upon herself to help Los Angeles knit itself back together.

She was a good person inside, she had lots of compassion, and she would show it. Sinking into despair was an act of the selfish.

She had missed the Edward Olmos–led broom cleanup of downtown because she was drinking Stoli in the queen sleigh bed.

But not anymore.

That was the old Bronwyn.

The new Bronwyn was going to take things one day at a time. She did not fully grasp the complexities of a multicultural society, but she believed that simple acts could help.

And so, the next day she got up, showered, and breakfasted.

One thing she, a person with an academic background, could offer was teaching expertise. And so she had volunteered through the Ethnic Studies department at UCLA—the one that had supplanted the Women's Studies department—to lead a workshop of Diversity 2000. It was a program for high school students in the

L.A. Unified School District, to help them become more aware of each other's differences.

But first she drove the rattling Geo out to Panorama City. This took her into a hot, flat, dusty part of the North San Fernando Valley, its streets littered with pawnshops, El Pollo Locos, and trash.

As she waited at a stoplight, she noticed that, to her right, a Latino man appeared to be sleeping in his parked car. A brown Pinto.

Sleeping in his car. Like Jonathan.

These things would usually depress her, but Bronwyn forced herself to try to ponder and love the colorful diversity of Los Angeles.

What a strange jumble, Bronwyn thought, driving up Van Nuys Boulevard. She was familiar with signs like "Taquería" and "Carnicería" and "Sabor Coca-Cola!"—a billboard from which a Latina gurgled. But now here was a tattered mini-mall with a Chicken Delight sign, a Sally For Nails sign and . . . what was that?

It was some weird language she had never seen before, with curlicues and apostrophes and exclamation marks. Good God! What was that?

Arabic? Pakistani? Urdu?

Where were all these people coming from? Who were they? Did they really consider Los Angeles, this smoggy grid, the land of opportunity? Just what had they come here to do?

She was very much used to the idea of a society of mixed races, but sometimes she wondered at the limits of this.

She thought about the time that she and Paul had eaten dinner at the Cuban restaurant Versailles. At one point, over their twin plates of Cuban roast pork, she'd looked across at the next table and seen not a nice Latino couple or a nice black couple or a nice Asian couple, but a Zulu. There was no other way to describe it. A Zulu. Straight out of *National Geographic*. Literally.

This was an almost seven-foot-tall bald man, jet-black from an equatorial sun. He wore feathers and beads and actually had an English muffin–size plate in his lip.

A plate in his lip. Right there at Versailles.

Not that it seemed to give him any problem. No. He calmly stabbed, cut, and chewed his garlic chicken, with easy enjoyment, and drank sangría. And even more paradoxically, the Zulu was speaking to his companion, an attractive well-groomed blond woman in a gray linen jacket, in one of the most beautifully modulated British accents Bronwyn had ever heard.

Bronwyn thought she could even detect a trace of the Hollywood bla bla bla. "Miramax . . . Cinemax . . . Richard Gere."

Bronwyn hadn't wanted to stare, but she almost couldn't help it. It was not morbid curiosity or social censure she felt, simply amazement. Flat-out amazement.

"A plate in his lip!" she whispered at Paul. "Right here in Santa Monica. Isn't that amazing? How is this all happening? What brings people here?"

While at that time she had felt only wonderment—even had had a bit of a giggle about it—now it all had a darker cast. Maybe the great social experiment of America had just resulted in too many people coming together too fast. Without rhyme. Without reason. Without a plan. And instead of fostering a rich new culture, it was all just a chaos.

She banished the thought, turned at the light.

LaForge Street had a neat but pinched appearance. Trash was stacked carefully, but lawns were totally dead. Cars were clean, but rusted—and unfashionable models at that: 1983 Chrysler LeBarons, brave if somewhat beaten Chevy Chevettes. In addition, the houses were painted slightly off-putting hues of lime green and pink.

Here it was: 18921 LaForge. The home of Concepción Rodríguez, maid, who Bronwyn was about to deliver her and Paul's old printer to. Why shouldn't Concepción's son Jesús have it, anyway? A bright kid of eleven, he loved to play with computers.

Service. Bronwyn could be of service to others.

Service. She kind of liked that word. Why not? The negation of self.

"Hallo, Mrs. Bronwyn!" Concepción cried out, greeting her at the door. "Oh thank you, thank you," she murmured in plaintive delight, taking the printer from her. "Jesús? Come and say thank you to Mrs. Bronwyn. Would you like coffee?"

Bronwyn did not particularly want coffee on this hot, dusty Saturday afternoon, but she was drawn into the house in spite of herself. She had that same hypnotized feeling she'd had at the trailer park in Florida. She felt herself in the presence of an incredible, eye-popping Cultural Difference.

Yes, 18921 LaForge was the kind of 1970s suburban tract house you saw so much of in the outlying regions of L.A. It was not unlike their old house in Tujunga, really. It had the sparkling cottage-cheese ceiling, sliding glass doors, aluminum windows; out back she could see part of a chain-link fence.

And yet . . . and yet. Well, first of all, there was a different color of carpet in every room. Shags, piles . . . It was as though the remnants of a Carpeteria sale had been dragged in here, then carefully cut into rectangles to more or less fit these rooms. The entryway featured a brown shag, the dining room was blood-red; beyond, a navy blue led into the hall.

A gilt-glass wall to their right, a hideous leftover from the seventies, instead of having been discreetly replaced with wood or brick or something less disco-y, had been decorated to maximal reflective effect with a Madonna and candles and plastic flowers foiled in silvery paper.

"We own!" Concepción told her, beaming.

"You own this?" Bronwyn was amazed.

"My family. Since 1982. We live here."

"No kidding." And of course, this house was in the Valley, she realized. Just like Kip Tarkanian had suggested. And the Rodríguezes bought it way back in '82—before the fall. If anyone was making money on their investment, it would be the Rod-ríguezes. That's perfect, she thought. That's just perfect.

"Here, here." Concepción happily held aside a—a hanging blanket . . . as though it were a marvelous brocade curtain leading to another wing of a fabulous summer palace.

They passed a small utility room . . . where a man in an under-shirt was sitting, on a mattress that barely fit into the room. Behind another hanging blanket was a tiny bedroom: she could barely glimpse beyond that a couple with a baby, and heard AM Mexican radio music playing. My God, Bronwyn thought, how many peo-ple live here?

They stepped finally into the crowded kitchen. Over the For-mica island, beyond the sliding glass doors, through a fragment of chain-link fence, Bronwyn could see an empty kidney-shaped swimming pool. With all kinds of potted plants in it—vegetables, it looked like. An elderly Latino, battered straw hat, his pants tied with string, poked into one of the pots with a trowel. Gardening. In a swimming pool. In Panorama City.

In the corner of the kitchen was little Jesús, and his computer. The computer was a filthy old Tandy, circa 1984. The back of the computer was open with wires hanging out of it. But when Bronwyn looked closer, she could see that some of the wires were hooked together with alligator clips. Perhaps there was method to this madness. It reminded her of the *Mad Max* films, where people cobbled strange new inventions together out of the scrapped machines of the twentieth century.

Jesús, in *E.T.* T-shirt, eyed the printer with ill-concealed interest.

"Oh Mrs. Bronwyn, thank you so," Concepción said winningly, as she put the kettle on. "Jesús—he know computers. But so difficult to buy new things. At school sometimes, he . . ."

As Concepción rattled on, Bronwyn's gaze floated around the kitchen. It was the domain of pack rats, of those who shopped thrift stores, searched dumpsters. Hanging off the sink, drying *Star Wars* towels. On the worn but clean counter, mega-sized bargain bags of corn chips. From the corner a clothesline hung, onto which colored pot holders were appended. Underneath that, a bunch of red chiles. And next to that . . .

Bronwyn stared at it, feeling the quiet click of recognition.

Bank envelopes. Rubber-banded together. In clear plastic bread sacks. Stacked against the toaster.

Where had she last seen that?

In the trailer park, of course. Hub and Dorothy. Husbanding their tiny, unfashionable scrap of land. Doing whatever . . . until money came out. Squeezing every penny out. Saving their dollars the old-fashioned way. Until their savings grew. And grew.

Immigrants! she thought. Immigrants who would bequeath their nest egg to the next generation. But what would the next generation do with it?

"Mami!" Jesús shrieked in sudden delight. There was a buzz, then the whine of the printer jumping into life.

There was an excited gathering around the printer, and then disappointment.

The printer was printing out weird apostrophes and signs that looked like Urdu.

"It is not compatible," Jesús said flatly.

"But it's an IBM," Bronwyn protested.

Jesús shook his head. "Microsoft," he said. "Microsoft."

"One thing we're learning as we Rebuild L.A.," Bronwyn read pleasantly off a card to the high school students and their teachers gathered before her in the Torrance gym, "is that even though we sometimes seem different from each other, at least outwardly— that is, even though we *look* different—we really have a lot of hidden similarities. So what we're going to do now is a Similarities Awareness Exercise which, we hope, will prove to you that while we are all different—like a big colorful quilt—we're really connected too in a lot of neat ways.

"First, let's break up into our continents. That's right. Go stand in the continent your ancestors came from."

"What if we came from two different continents?" a girl in pigtails and blue glasses piped up, puffed with a certain sense of martyrdom.

"Well, pick the one you're most closely affiliated with. You think. As it stands now."

Obediently, like sheep, everyone moved into their groups. Soon all the black people were standing together—the teachers and their mostly female students—politely standing together and talking. To the other side of the gym stood the Latinos. One girl at the front wore a Madonna "Like a Virgin" sweatshirt. By far the largest group—perhaps twice as large as the others—was the whites, who stood in "Europe."

The only odd situation was Asia. Standing there were two obviously Asian girls, one tall, one short, the latter clad in a truly hideous red and green Christmas sweater. It bore the frantic legend "Noel Noel Noel!!!" across the chest, under which sailed a flotilla of sequined teddy bears with mouths wide open à la Edvard Munch's *The Scream*. Which was all fine.

But now, lumbering toward the two girls, eagerly as Columbus arriving in his splendid boats to a wonderful new land, were two obviously Caucasian teachers. They were beaming and fortyish, one wearing Birkenstocks and a Greenpeace sweatshirt.

"Uh, that is Asia," Bronwyn said. "Are you Asian?"

"Why yes!" Greenpeace Sweatshirt informed her happily, pointing to her partner. "At least she is."

"I am one-sixteenth descended from Cherokee Indians," the other offered, "and the Indians originally came over from Asia across the Bering Strait . . ."

"So she feels most strongly affiliated with Asia! And I do too," Greenpeace added, "at least spiritually."

The two Asian girls scowled at them.

The next division was East Coast, Middle America, West Coast—where did your family originate from?

Here almost the whole gym stood on the West Coast. There was not much of interest there.

"Oh yes!" Bronwyn cried out. "I almost forgot. Talk amongst yourselves and find three things everyone likes or agrees on."

A bit disgruntled that the exercise was rolling out in such a haphazard manner, with the leader forgetting instructions from one moment to the next, the groups obeyed.

But getting over a hundred people, including many teenagers who looked like they needed a lunch break, involved in a group dialogue was an arduous task. "We all like the beach!" someone called out at some point. "I like to water-ski!" another called out. "How about hiking?" But the voices were few and disparate, and tentative in their conviction of how well they represented the whole.

Murmuring grew among the clans, some conversation expressing puzzlement with where this was going; some, happy conversation on other topics entirely.

"What religion were you born into?" was the next question.

Bronwyn gestured at the different islands. "Catholic here, Protestants here, Christians here—"

"Aren't Protestants Christians?" someone yelled out.

"Yes!"

The Latino kids were mostly headed toward Catholic, but aside from that, there was no pattern at all. In the middle of the room was a large, chaotic group of cool kids—dreadlocks, tie-dyed T-shirts—who were calling themselves "agnostic."

"But were you *born* agnostic?" one teacher in an orange cardigan was pointing out. "The question is, what religion were you *born* into?"

But now Bronwyn noticed a strange vibe occurring among the "Christians." They were all looking at each other with glowing, if somewhat accusing, faces. "Have you accepted the Lord Jesus

Christ as your Savior?" one heavy teen with the worst skin she had ever seen accosted another. "*I* just did last year."

"But were you *born* that?" Bronwyn called out.

"I was born again, if that's what you mean," he persisted, luminous in the truth of it.

"We all love the Lord Jesus Christ!" the Christians were all calling out, quite correctly, as their similarity. "We all love the Lord Jesus Christ!"

"I think there's some confusion," put in another teacher. "This is the religion you were born into, not the one you chose."

Her voice rising with hysteria, Bronwyn put her hands up and cried out, "Okay, okay—stand in the religion you chose!"

Now a few Catholics came over to Christian, a few Jews went over to agnostic, two agnostic kids with punk hair walked over to Buddhist, and one pale Baptist—blond page boy, neat cardigan, wraparound floral skirt—walked proudly over to Jew and stood right in the front, beaming.

"What happened to *her*?" a large black woman—"Baptist"—asked loudly.

"See! Our group got bigger! Our group got bigger!" the excitable teen with the bad skin shouted.

"Your similarities?" Bronwyn asked nervously.

"We're going to heaven and they're going to hell!" the Christians piped up humorously, but with a certain edge.

"Okay, okay—" Bronwyn rushed in, trying to bring order to the gym. "Let's get off that. Let's get to something more straightforward. Income! Income! Are your families high-income, middle-income, low-income?"

"What's the break-off point?" someone queried.

There was no information about that in the index cards.

"Well, you decide!" Bronwyn called out, smiling weakly. "You decide! However that feels for you!"

Here all the teachers angrily marched to low-income. "Thanks to Proposition Thirteen!" one bearded teacher in shorts and sandals declared. "We haven't had a pay raise in eight years! Of course they still have funds to pay for goofy programs like this. Thanks a lot!" He turned and pointed to Bronwyn, who quailed on her chair. "Thanks a lot!"

The high-incomes were a small group of whites who tried to look very casual. But one could tell they felt pretty good about being the high-income people. Their tennis shoes *were* just a bit newer and cleaner than the rest of the room's. Two of the teachers stood there, but they were white women and obviously independently wealthy. Resentments were building.

"We're poor!" One humorous black teen punched his fist in the air. "And we're proud!"

"Yeah whitey!" one of the poor white students called out gamely, also punching his fist upward.

"Democrat or Republican?" Bronwyn squeaked, looking at her index card.

A few middle-class whites joined the high-income whites, with their Nikes and gold chains and nice haircuts. Even though they were the smaller, more privileged group, they still weren't afraid to be vocal.

When the Democrats cried out: "We're going to put our man Bill in office!" the Republicans booed hypnotically, as though at a sports event: "Slick Willie! Slick Willie! Slick Willie!"

When Bronwyn gave the final instruction—"Please stand in the ethnic group you feel yourself most closely affiliated with"— all hell broke loose.

"I am tired of being categorized by my race!" the large black Baptist woman cried out. "Enough already! We make too many categories as it is!"

"White? White? I'm sick of being called white!" the bearded teacher in shorts and sandals yelled. "My ancestors were Jews from Czechoslovakia! We have about as much in common with the British or Scottish as we do with the Swahilis! I'm tired of being lumped together like this!"

"This is a stupid exercise!" a youth in dreadlocks and a tie-dyed T-shirt pointed out. "It's really regressive! It puts people into artificial boxes that maybe they don't feel are—"

Bronwyn's face had flamed red. "No, no, no," she stumbled. "That's exactly the point of this exercise! That these categories are all arbitrary and that they can change! We can be pulled together by as many categories as we're separated by!"

But even as she said this, she knew it was wrong. The white high-income Christian Republicans, for instance, had become the most hated group in the room. They never mingled with anyone in any other category.

"I can't believe the government is spending money on this!" the bearded teacher yelled. It makes me furious!"

Bronwyn felt totally wrecked.

The exercise—led by her—was a disaster.

The only thing she had to offer was compassion for the downtrodden, compassion that for years had served her in good stead. It had been something she could count on, rely on, depend on. It was the center, the root of her personality—the thing that anchored all of her foibles. Or so she had believed.

But in this brave new world, her compassion was a gift no one could use. Or even wanted.

The elevator doors opened.

There stood the two Asian girls, the tall one and the short one, bespectacled, morose, in her "Noel Noel Noel!!!" sweater. It was one of the most defiantly ugly sweaters Bronwyn had ever seen.

In spite of herself, she felt a stab of pity for a teenager who would be forced to wear such an ugly sweater.

Poor kid, having to go to school looking like that, so square, an outsider, in plastic sandals, when all the other girls were in cool flannel shirts and mascara and . . .

But was this truly pity, or was this *condescension*? Was this *scorn*?

And when Bronwyn truly examined herself, she realized she probably did condescend rather than pity people. Sometimes. So she busied herself in helping them, bustling about with activity, to stanch the voice, the voice of the ego, the voice that screamed, Aren't you glad you're *better* than them? You're woeful, yes, but not quite so woeful as this tattered person . . . and that gives you comfort, doesn't it?

But no. She closed her eyes.

She honestly wished this girl well. She honestly did. She truly wished she could give this little Asian girl a nicer sweater. She truly wished she could say, "Hey. Here's a nice tailored black sweater that will set off your hair beautifully, and here are some sleek pleated pants from Ann Taylor that . . ."

But perhaps this girl would not want these things. Perhaps she liked her Christmas sweater.

Perhaps the girl did not even speak English. Perhaps she would be irate that Bronwyn did not speak to her in her own language. That was true: Bronwyn was much too English-centered. But Chinese! Bronwyn knew a little Spanish, but no Chinese. No Chinese. Then again, she did. Yes, she did. One phrase . . .

"Nee how ma?" Bronwyn murmured brokenly to the girl. *"Nee how ma?"*

"We may all look alike, but we don't all speak alike!" the taller Asian suddenly spat out.

The hate covered Bronwyn like a flame.

"The self-loathing of you, these liberal whites," the tall Asian went on. "Why do you fawn over us so? We are not your long-lost friends. We are not your family. Spend time with your own kind! Go to Cub Scout meetings! Celebrate your own culture! Read British poetry! Get off me! Get off me! Get off me!"

Bronwyn closed her eyes, continued to take it. And . . .

"Nee how ma," she kept whispering woodenly, as if it were some kind of futile Hail Mary. *"Nee how ma?"*

bon voyage

Colin Martin's plans to leave Los Angeles had been in motion long before "the L.A. uprising," as he called it.

Although of course, he felt terrible about having to go.

"The timing couldn't be worse," Colin was saying to the group gathered on his lawn for one last event—his bon voyage party. "Now's the time for people to stay in L.A. to help rebuild it. My office at ABC has already donated sixty thousand dollars to the Rebuild L.A. fund. I figure it's the least we can do. But of course it's never enough." He sighed. "It's never enough."

He shook his head. What was done was done. Last February, in that calm, quiet, gearwheeled world of his, moving serenely above the confused shamblings of a battered city, he had given notice at ABC, put his house up for sale, and booked his flight out of L.A.

Destination: Boulder, Colorado.

To spend a few years quietly growing vegetables, composting, doing a bit of consulting for the company, and . . .

Writing . . .

His novel.

"It's a legal thriller based on some of the experiences I had in my law days. Kind of in the John Grisham vein. But there's a spiritual side to it too, in a subtle way . . ."

Because Colin Martin was the type of person fortune smiled upon, he had even managed to get a sizable advance on his book.

Which was, of course, the way things worked in this world, Bronwyn thought grimly. In dark sunglasses, she stood off to the edge of the group, wordless, personality-less, incognito . . . a veritable shell of her former bustling self.

Here Colin Martin had already been making six figures a year, she figured, he had equity and CDs and T-bills and whatnot in the bank, and now that he was taking it upon himself to write a novel, nothing would do but for publishers to throw even more money at him. Money he had so much of, he could even dispense it to the poor—who would not spit on him, as they did on Bronwyn, but would honor him with plaques and speeches and touchingly homespun needlepoint samplers.

Not that Colin's charity extended everywhere, of course. Because finally, when push came to shove, Colin had turned down Paul's material. But in a really nice way. The door was still open. Etc., etc. A messenger had sent it back with a note that said:

> Paul,
> There's a little too much dialogue here—
> And too much description—
> I'd love to see the next one though—
> C.M.

And so, at this point, Bronwyn and Paul couldn't afford to leave Los Angeles—the city that had turned its back on them, the city that loathed them. They could not afford to buy an ecologically correct palace in Colorado and grow vegetables and write uplifting books and still have money left over to donate generously to gang members so they could build their own basketball courts in South Central. They did not even have a clear $300 to heal their car.

Not that anyone like Colin Martin would ever leave L.A. just because of the riots. He'd never stoop to the low raw panic of it. Even though in a particularly down moment, Bronwyn had been half tempted to scrawl "White flight!" on her bon voyage card. A flight she herself would not be ashamed to take, given the opportunity. Shame? What was shame anymore?

"But television . . . Hollywood?" someone was saying. "Won't you miss it?"

"It's just that I'm thirty-three now—I feel that my values are changing—" Colin looked apologetic about it—about daring to have something as old-fashioned as values.

Bronwyn could only stare as she quaffed mug after mug of imported beer (chased with a kind of rare vodka Colin had unearthed on a recent trip to East Germany, now that the Wall was down). She studied his beige, heavy-ribbed V-neck sweater, stonewashed jeans, and funny little mukluks—mukluks that she now knew were quite expensive. How smoothly he had moved beyond Crate & Barrel–hood and into everything L. L. Bean. He was looking blond and rugged and unexpectedly boyish in a poetic Keats way.

"You know," Colin sighed. "Clean air, mountains, a place where you can walk across a field in the middle of the night and look up at the stars—that's something that looks really good to me right now. It's just that the eighties were so crazy," he continued, after a moment, frowning. "The money we'd pour out on restaurants alone . . ."

"Hear, hear." Doug, one of his law cronies in shirtsleeves, raised his glass.

"I mean, who needs to spend a hundred and fifty bucks on a single meal? It was just nuts! French food—how we used to think that was the be-all and end-all to everything."

French food. Champagne. Oysters. Foie gras. The haunches of pampered young cattle in a delectable cream sauce. White table-cloths. Silver candlesticks. It was not that Bronwyn wanted such things per se. It was that she wished she'd had a chance to at least grandly say no to them . . . like Colin was doing now.

Because all these wonderful things were part of the party . . . the big party that everyone said was the eighties. The party that was now over. The party she and Paul had never been invited to in the first place.

Bronwyn had an image of herself as this hunched-over figure, a dark crow on this lawn, reaching out a claw to grab one of those shivering oysters she had never tasted—and of that claw some-how always being slapped away: "No, Bronwyn! You can't have that! That's so horribly eighties!"

"But what are you going to do with your beautiful house?" a worried, even faintly hysterical female voice cried out. Bronwyn turned. It was Chelsea, the hundred-year-old Bohemian, in a saggy kind of red velvet Renaissance hat. Still the crow's-feet. Still the too-dark purple lipstick. Still the wrinkled scarf.

Boho. Hobo.

Hm. Bronwyn had never considered how closely these words were related.

"Fortunately . . ." Colin admitted. She noted how often he

began his responses with that word. "Fortunately, I *did* find a buyer right away, who gave me pretty close to my asking price."

"Really!" Doug erupted. "In *this* market?"

"I think I got out just before things really began to plunge." Colin was rueful, embarrassed about this fact.

"Real estate values are dropping, like, ten thousand a month!" Doug murmured in amazement, turning to the group.

"Tell me about it," a tanned older blonde in a white muslin dress put in, in a hushed voice. "The bottom has dropped out of the market. The riots didn't exactly help matters."

"Particularly in the center of town, near where the disturbances happened," her husband added. "Forget about it. People are getting out in droves."

In her mind's eye, Bronwyn saw a huge blue tsunami curling over, her and Paul being sucked down into its maw like little straw dolls. It seemed to her that their timing had always been off. They were always on the underside of the wave instead of on the crest, and were thus constantly being crushed by the forces of the tides.

"For me, I think it was just luck," Colin revealed. "I'd met my buyer through my old law firm . . . an Armenian expatriate who'd been in the antique business . . ."

"A lot of them have quite a bit of money, quite a bit," Doug added, for the elucidation of all, taking another pull of his lager.

"The dropping of the Iron Curtain was very good for them—"

"Not to mention for the Russians. Have you seen how much money they seem to be throwing around these days?"

"As opposed to the Japanese. They're pulling out of downtown like you wouldn't believe. One of our clients . . ."

The Armenians. The Russians. Bronwyn closed her eyes. Who could keep track? You had all these foreign peoples coming into

America—who could tell which were the wealth-bearing ones, which the wealth-sapping ones? Five years ago, who would have known to throw their lot in with the Russians? They were the people in babushkas, pushing along wheelbarrows, grunting in potato fields. Now suddenly they were wealthy as Croesus, dancing in L.A. nightclubs in Guess? jeans and gold chains, buying up a storm.

The Japanese, on the other hand, the Japanese. In the eighties, they'd been the sure thing. The yen's value was in the sky, they bought up one gleaming high-rise in downtown after the other: Sumitomo, Matsushita, Sanyo . . . The names—Bronwyn's view from her living room—jingled across her brain like a karaoke song.

But now, in late 1992, the Japanese were dirt, they were nothing, they were on the run. The high-rises were emptying out, there were foreclosures. Like the tide, they were retreating. Hastily. The Japanese, of course, were the folks who owned her own building, Symphony Towers. Ach. Bronwyn's head slumped forward onto her chest for a moment. Who would have known that the Japanese . . . would become destitute!

That trail of brave pioneers—immigrants—heading toward Los Angeles with their suitcases and laptop computers and woks and menorahs and sombreros . . . swelling the wealth, swelling the wealth of Los Angeles such that there was a gold mine in the center of the city. A gold mine that radiated outward, warming those closest to it . . .

How wrong she had been, how pathetically, even comically wrong she had been about everything. Ha.

"Did you buy a new place then?" the blonde said, cutting to the chase. "Did you buy something in Colorado?"

"Well, I did," Colin admitted. He hesitated, as though not wanting to go on.

"Well?" the blonde persisted.

The words came out in a controlled monotone.

"Twenty-five acres, including even a creek—full of trout—that winds its way through the back fields. It's a four-bedroom house—three stories, wood, remodeled, skylights, an attic." He shook his head, humbly boyish, found out. "It's great, it's completely great. Got a pretty good deal on it . . ." He wasn't going to say exactly how good a deal, but really pretty good.

"Twenty-five acres!" Doug exploded.

"Well, it's too quiet of course," Colin put in quickly. "I mean, Boulder isn't for everyone."

There were murmurs of assent, but they lacked energy. Everyone looked beaten, tired. To the east, free of the roiling black smoke of riots, everyone was seeing Boulder, Colorado, in their mind's eye—its snowy white mountains rising pristine, gleaming against stunning azure skies. In fetid L.A. were drooping real estate prices, trash-filled streets, and angry blacks like Maxine Waters, brows knit, jabbing her energetic forefinger at everyone not black and not in a slum.

Damn, I wish I had the money to get out of here, people were thinking.

"Well, I'm going to make the best of staying in fabulous L.A.," a slim, goateed young man in a Hawaiian shirt suddenly put out, boldly. "I think things are just starting to get interesting!"

"Interesting. Sure," someone replied.

"I've decided that it's better to get with the program than fight it," Hawaiian Shirt continued cheerily. "Forget AA, twelve-step programs, rolfing. I'm taking a class at the Learning Annex that's teaching me to get in touch with my *inner tagger.*"

"Oh really?" Chelsea asked. "That's interesting—"

"It's a joke," Doug snapped at her. "It's like 'inner child.' But with a certain cholo twist."

"I'm thinking positively. In the Valley, where I'm from," Hawaiian Shirt pushed on, "there *were* no riots. We went to bed early that night. Or we watched it on TV. In fact . . ."

He looked around the group, his goatee trembling with fun.

"In fact, for us the riots were largely a televised event. Some of us were wondering if it even took place at all!"

There were cries of outrage, some unhappy laughter, people turning to help themselves to more lager, or to more vodka, as the case might be.

"That's absurd!" Chelsea exclaimed, stung.

"Well, were you there?" Hawaiian Shirt challenged.

Chelsea balked. "Well no . . ." Her face became animated again. "But I could see smoke!"

He shrugged. "Flares. A propmaster set them off. So what?"

"But all those people helping Edward James Olmos clean it up the next day," Doug pointed out. "I had a friend who—"

"Were *you* there?" Hawaiian Shirt probed. "Did *you* see the wreckage?"

Doug just gave a short laugh, shook his head.

"I'm thinking the whole thing was like *Capricorn One,*" Hawaiian Shirt was continuing. "Remember *Capricorn One*—where they staged a moon landing that was completely fake? They did it via television. Hal Holbrook. In my world, you see, the riots may never have happened!"

"Oh my God," the blonde said.

"How many of us were actually there? None! How many of us even know where a 118th and Crenshaw is? No one! How do we know these places even exist? I'm thinking maybe it was a television stunt put on by the news networks. Think of their ratings . . . through the roof!"

The kitchen.

Bronwyn stepped into it.

She let out her breath—and her bitterness—with a sigh, as her eyes traced one last time over . . .

The blue and white tile. The skylights, letting in the gorgeous golden light of the late afternoon.

The gorgeous golden light that was yellow with regret. As in the end of summer. As in the last glass of red wine drunk at the picnic table. As in the last story told, the laughter fading, the smiles dying from lips, the ending of the dream. The trees reddening in the sunset, the air just beginning to chill. Shadows spilled across the butcher-block center island, the hanging burnished copper pans, the herb garden twisting in the corner . . .

Colin appeared with a tray.

"Colorado?" Bronwyn asked him. "Huh?"

He smiled, nodded, shrugged his shoulders. Turned.

They leaned against the counter together, gazing upon Colin's perfect kitchen.

"Leave it all behind, huh?" she said.

His mouth sagged, slightly petulant.

For just a moment, he lost his goldenness, his manliness, his height.

For just a moment, she saw a flash of the young Colin, the awkward Colin, the shy Colin, the Colin of the awful plaid cardigans.

"You know, Bronwyn, we could have . . . dated once. Maybe things would have turned out a little bit differently for you."

His voice dropped a little.

"If you wanted to, you could be leaving too."

"I can't tell you how much I would love to do that," she said, feelingly caught by the thought. "Farmhouse, beautiful green fields, clean mountains, creek . . ."

"I know you, Bronwyn. I know that you would love it. You hate this city. You've always hated it. And now look what L.A.'s becoming. It's impossible. It's impossible even if you want to do right, if you try to do right, try to do everything right."

She closed her eyes, feeling another wave of exhaustion wash over her.

"Wouldn't you like to start completely over?"

She would. She would. The thought of never having to fight her way again across the 101 seemed wonderful. Of no longer being a prisoner of Symphony Towers—of no longer having to stand at the prow of her white ocean liner, look out at the glassy high-rises, and have that sick feeling in the pit of her stomach, the sick feeling that as each day progressed they were sinking farther and farther in debt. That there was a big crater pit where their future should be.

She would love Colorado. She knew she would love it. She imagined Colin's wonderful wooden house. It would be warmly decorated, every brand-new—and yet ecologically correct— appliance humming along; the air would smell crisp and clean in the morning, a rich roast-coffee aroma floating in from the kitchen.

Inspiration would be new there. Maybe she'd go back to the Colonial American women poets, finish her thesis. Write a new thesis. Go into dried flower design. Become queen of the beet fair. Start hand-painting chairs and selling them. Or giving them away, to friends and charities. Sharing things. Rag dolls, straw baskets, canned fruit. She imagined large-paned windows flanking a wooden upstairs office with large drafting tables for projects and . . .

Christmases would be wonderful—snowing, warm, the crunch of pine. Spring would be wonderful. Summer would be wonderful. There would be seasons—not the grating sameness of L.A., every season punctuated by the glint of car metal, the exhaust, the trash, the homeless. It would be far from hate. There would only be the cool whisper of nature there. It would be perfect.

But that was the problem. It was perfect.

Everything Bronwyn had imagined in her life that was perfect was not real.

It was all a mirage.

Every life that Bronwyn had ever been able to describe, as clear to her as movie plots . . . all turned out to be a mirage.

The sixties . . . which for her had turned out to be nothing but a VW bus that kept breaking down.

The Bohemian lifestyle . . . a total sham, something pre-processed, packaged, marketed, and even discounted for the losers who still believed in it.

Her Connecticut white clapboard farmhouse . . . At that exact moment the farmhouse was probably housing a small tribe of Ph.D.s in Native American studies. The ones who had gotten her job at Westbury College. They were probably sleeping on the floor in blankets, due to a set of complicated religious beliefs, and creating a large pot of spattering lentil and corn soup.

Who had the real farmhouse? Colin Martin. Not a farmer. A lawyer. And where had he had it? In downtown Pasadena. Not because he'd had good harvests, but because he'd made money in real estate. And to add to the irony, now that he was moving to Colorado, where they actually had farms, he was going to be living in a mansion.

The fact being that in Bronwyn's life, for whatever reason, the only things that would ever be real were not the perfect things but the imperfect ones. The fearful, the ugly, the unmatched, the tattered, the battered, the worn.

And on realizing that, for the first time in her life Bronwyn glimpsed the true shape, texture, and measure of Adulthood. And saw that the landscape unfolding before her was not a neatly laid-out grid, neat as the miniature American town of a trailer park, with well-planned programs, curriculums, and mentors. No, Adulthood was a huge alien landmass with no guideposts, street-lights, or maps. No rules, no safeguards, and no insurance.

The knowledge of it—of this great formless void of unknowing—left her feeling small and humble, as humble as a twelve-year-old. The bright little world of school and classes and cheerful house parties and chili recipes and favorite battered records and comical beanbag chairs and happy, exact plans for the future was all in the past. It was packed and sealed up in a box called Youth. From now on, over the decades that stretched ahead, she would be feeling her way in the dark, step by step.

"I can't leave," was what came out in a croak.

It was a simple statement, but true. And in saying so, she remembered the one thing she was sure *would* be in her life. But the thought did not give her its accustomed comfort. On the contrary, it gave her a new, dawning sense of overwhelming responsibility and dread. She wanted to cry with the despair of it:

"Because Paul is here. Paul. My life . . . is with Paul."

baywatching

That morning, Bronwyn was awoken not by NPR, not by her alarm clock, not by sirens, but by Paul. He was stroking her hair back with both hands. For a split second, she did not recognize this man behind the new wire-rims, having known Paul for so many years as the Elvis Costello glasses guy. But of course, the serious eyes were the same, always the same, dreadfully the same.

"Bronwyn?" he asked.

"Hm," she grunted.

"I've been fired by Zibby Tanaka. But it's okay," he amended quickly. "They're going to give me a severance check. It's not as much as I would have gotten paid if I'd worked all the way through the end of the contract, but well . . ." He pushed up his glasses with one hand. "It'll have to do. It'll have to do for now."

That was the phrase Paul's parents always used, when pushing across the kitchen table such minor matters as their life savings. "It'll have to do for now." And looking at him now, slumped on the edge of the bed, Bronwyn saw in Paul, for the first time, a certain heaviness, a knitting of the brow, a weariness in the shoulders, a tightness of jaw. It was Hub's weariness. It was Hub.

And with each passing year, Paul would only become more so. Yes. That was the secret of their lives. With each passing year, both he and she would become more and more like their suburban parents.

And that was the best they could hope for. That was the zenith of their potential.

They would reach the middle class if they were lucky.

At this point, jobless, childless, cashless, soon to be homeless, they were rather behind schedule.

"I mean, sometimes they don't even give you severance checks on these film deals," Paul pressed on, determined to put a positive spin on things.

There was a beat.

"I guess that's . . . good news then," she said flatly. "Hurray."

"So . . ." he wondered, tucking a tendril of hair behind her ear. He attempted a smile, in a heroic effort to shift the tenor of the conversation. "You want to do something today? Go out somewhere?"

"Where?" she asked. "Where do unemployed people go on Monday mornings?"

"We could go . . . to the beach," he tried. "It's free."

She said nothing.

"We could go to the beach," he repeated softly, even sadly. "You and I."

You and I. It was like the title of some tune popular in the twenties, something that people would listen to on an old tinny radio. Ghostly, nostalgic, quaint, it was reminiscent of a colorful joyous time, a time of people in top hats and fox furs crowded and laughing in restaurants, a time before everything fell. A lyric that should be on a sad little card in a museum. Families and their children would read the card and look into a diorama and feel very sorry.

Because in the diorama, Bronwyn thought, would be pictured the tattered, faded little tribe from Tujunga: the two dolls Bronwyn and Paul forever frozen, eyebrows theatrically arched, arms lifted, striking positions of meager drama in their neat, pathetically hopeful kitchen in Symphony Towers, with the washed-pine table and the beeswax candles and the twigs.

"The beach," she repeated, dull.

But because, in fact, they had nothing else to do, nothing else on their schedules—it was that simple—the beach was what they eventually set out for . . .

But where was it? Even though they had been living together in L.A. for seven years, neither Bronwyn nor Paul had any idea how to get there. They knew where the sea was, but were unclear as to how one actually got onto the sand.

So their first stop was at the Trader Joe's on National, to pick up refreshments and instructions.

Thus stocked, saying very little to each other, they continued west on the 10 through this gray, oppressive, and yet uncomfortably warmish L.A. day, the air heavy, almost metallic, with filth. The Geo Futura was leaking oil like a sieve. They had given over to it, stopped fighting it, surrendered to the fact that to keep the Futura running you had to pour a new can of oil in it every day, $4.99 a pop. The chassis shuddered when one downshifted. The left blinker had stopped blinking. The air conditioner blasted in something that smelled like old carpet. But these were minor things, all somehow falling beyond the warranty, when the fine print was studied.

Twenty minutes later, they arrived at the beach at Chautauqua. They paid $5 to park. There was no problem finding a spot. It was a weekday, after all. Most people were working.

Blinking like lizards under a weak sun, eyes fixed suspiciously on gray waves, they set foot upon the alien territory of the beach, stumbling over the dunes as their shoes filled with sand.

Eventually they stopped. They set their things down uncertainly. They did not own bathing suits. In their sweaters and pants, they were strangers among the beach people.

Paul had bought a bottle of $1.99 Trader Joe's Merlot, the weakest vintage known to man, a purplish broth of discarded grapes—all they could afford, even on the Visa—and a slightly bent baguette. He set them out on a towel.

"A jug of wine, a loaf of bread, and thou," he said.

"Hm," Bronwyn said.

They sloshed the thin purplish broth into paper cups and sat, hunched over, on the beach.

Before them, a gaggle of gaily dressed Latino toddlers played on the sand. Beyond were two Asian girls in Porsche sunglasses and string bikinis, reading. Beyond that, a busload of what appeared to be African-American schoolchildren out on a field trip.

Farther down the beach, cordoned off behind a circle of trucks protective and implacable as covered wagons, a film crew was shooting an episode of *Baywatch*. You could tell because that's what it said on the side of the trucks, emblazoned in yellow-and-orange logos. Occasionally one could get a glimpse of distant Caucasian Rollerbladers, the flight of a beach ball, a flip of blond hair.

It was a totally discordant panorama, a conjunction of unlike elements that would only come together in one city in the world . . .

Bronwyn sighed.

It was at that moment that she had the overwhelming sensation that Los Angeles was like a thing that happened to them a long time ago. She was losing hold of the details of what had brought them here, what they had wanted to do, what they had wanted to become.

All she knew was that she and Paul were crouched here, in their sweaters, on a blasted beach. All she knew was that she was so tired her bones ached.

They continued to sip the bargain Merlot from Dixie Cups, staining their teeth purple.

Eventually, she stretched back on the towel, closed her eyes.

Dimly, she became aware of Paul settling back next to her, also bone tired, her fellow patient lying etherized upon the warm table of the beach.

She felt a breeze roil around her.

And the sun.

Though as a dyed-in-the-wool Bohemian, clad perennially in black, the sun had seemed to her evil, the enemy, the sign of everything that was brainless in Southern California, she had to admit that it was, in fact, a warm pleasant feeling upon her.

Gradually she became aware of the lap of the waves, the faint shouts of the children.

The sun, the sun.

And because there was nothing else to do, she rolled over and stole her arms around her fellow, such as he was, because his was the body that was still there.

He lay quiet and let her.

Then she tilted her chin up.

She at first planned to make it a short kiss, a peck, the sorrowful squeeze of a hand one member of a couple gives another before entering the ICU.

But it was so pleasant, with the sun and the waves, she decided to linger with it, stay awhile longer. She settled her body in closer to his.

In fact, just for the hell of it, because they had no plans that day, because they had nowhere else to go, Bronwyn began to explore Paul's face . . .

His face . . .

Her mind floated back to Paul's face as it was the first time she'd seen him twelve years ago at that college dorm party at San Jose State. A lamp fell somewhere, streamers filled the air, freshmen heads were screaming, ZZ Top was on the stereo. Paul's face was slightly thinner then, a boy's face really, not serious at all. She had the memory of him being impossibly animated, talking to a million people, turning his head to one person and then another, a welter of thoughts and expressions streaking over him.

She remembered the curve of Paul's back—and it always was curved, always had been, even at twenty. She remembered the way that back, in a worn T-shirt, would curve over in a slump on any couch he sat on. She remembered it particularly vividly from Tujunga, in the mornings, the dust motes floating over him, as Paul drank his coffee in his karate pants, reading his paper and his books and his magazines so intensely, his big black glasses perched on his nose, in such full absorption, like a Tibetan monk.

She remembered his arms, his legs . . .

Such familiar, once so beloved terrain Paul's body was. As Bronwyn went over it, eyes now closed because she knew it, knew it so well . . . it all began to drift back to her.

The country lanes of him. The humble cottages. The gentle pastoral lands. The homeland long forgotten.

It was beloved, yes, but it was all brown and faded, as though in an aging twenties photograph.

"You know that I love you," Bronwyn murmured, suddenly feeling a poetic sense not of passion but of . . . duty. "You know that. I'm sure you sometimes forget. I mean, *I* forget."

Paul nodded. He leaned up on one arm. "You know what I was thinking this morning?"

"Hm?"

"You know how we always said we'd get married when I made my first sale?"

She nodded her head. That whole era—of excited talk, plans, enthusiasm—seemed so far in the past.

His words came out jaggedly, in a tumble.

"Well, technically I did make a sale. I wrote a film. It's in production. I got paid. Never mind if I got fired as well. When you look at the broadest outlines of it, the requirements are filled."

"Well . . . that's true," Bronwyn said slowly. She didn't want to hurt Paul, but neither was she really in the mood for a major romance discussion.

"So," he went doggedly on, "I think we should get married. Soon."

Bronwyn said nothing, watching the breeze ruffle the hair on his forehead.

He squeezed her elbow. His expression became sly.

"So you can get on my health insurance."

This drew her attention.

She laughed bitterly. "What health insurance?"

"It turns out that under the Diversity 2000 plan, I have health insurance." He looked away, studiously casual. "I got this big package of forms in the mail last Friday. The plan continues on for the rest of the year regardless of my situation with Zibby Tanaka. I've already paid enough into the fund.

"And my dependents are covered too. Which includes my . . . wife."

"What?"

Bronwyn sat up, unable to believe her ears. They had never had health insurance. And yet, this had the ring of truth . . .

As it was, neither of them had been to the doctor in five years. Every so often, when the guilt became too great, they'd scuttle furtively in to get their teeth cleaned at "Dr. Campbell, Credit Dentist." It was a mini-mall place so battered that even the "i" was missing on the sign, so that it said, "Dr. Campbell, Credit Dent st"—which always called to Bronwyn's mind someone trying to smile even though a tooth had been knocked out.

"What company is . . ." she fumbled.

"Blue Cross," Paul murmured.

Her voice sailed high in amazement. "Blue Cross?"

He stroked her arm, knowing his message was getting through. "Blue Cross. The best. The Rolls-Royce of health insurance. We can get checkups. We can get glasses. We can get root canals. We can even get . . ." He grinned. "Prescription drugs."

"Oh my God!" Insanely, Bronwyn felt a flow of warmth over her, like a gigantic comforter. It was not so much the draw of the free root canal, of course, but the sense of caring . . . That someone, Blue Cross, was going to be like this great mother to them who chucked you under the chin and said, "Honey? I really want you to go in and get some glasses. It's on me."

"It's totally weird," Bronwyn said, wonderingly, "but this is making me actually . . . feel happy. I never thought we would be people . . . with health insurance—"

"We can get sick now!" Paul enthused. "We can—"

"It's like we're adults or something! Like maybe we're not losers after all." She closed her eyes in the sun, feeling the smile of it all over her. "It's wonderful."

"Don't you think it would be kind of romantic to get married today, on a Monday morning, when all the other drones are at work?" Paul persisted. "It could be kind of artistic, kind of Bohemian. Kind of . . . *filmic*."

"But how . . ." She tugged at his arm, in a gesture almost childlike. "Don't you need a marriage license?"

"They cost thirty dollars," he replied. "That we have. It's probably all we have. But isn't that kind of cool . . . spending the last of our money on ourselves?" He made a mock muscle with his arm, adopted his best Maynard G. Krebs accent. "We're artists, baby. We're going to give it to the man. And we're going to do it for . . . for Blue Cross."

Bronwyn smiled again at the simplicity of it. It was the perfectly irresponsible—and yet, ironically, *responsible*—thing to do, the first Monday of one's unemployment.

And so, an hour later, Paul and Bronwyn were parking at the Los Angeles County Courthouse. Paul made a mental note of their surroundings. "Maybe later we can go to the *taquería*," he joked. "Sure," she replied. "We have time."

She kept her voice gay, but in fact was feeling slightly dampened by the scene ahead of them. This had started off as a fun romp, but in fact, what lay beyond seemed not *filmic* at all but rather real, grim, a bit too grittily Zola-esque.

They mounted the trash-scattered stairs into the gray government building. They took their place in line behind the many improverished Latinos—the women with their big soft fleshy brown arms and hair like Las Vegas fright wigs, the squalling children in their perpetually soiled hot-pink party dresses. The song of an ice cream truck smeared by. From somewhere deep in the bowels of the building, a Mexican radio station murmured.

Along the wall was painted a mural of some stiff-muscled Indians, feathers drooping, impotently holding toy-size spears, looking over what eventually would become the City of Los Angeles. Their gazes were morose—a people whose prospects looked, at best, disappointing.

"I know just how they feel," Paul said. He leaned into her ear. "Health insurance. Just keep your mind focused on that."

A child ahead of them with a nose ring and curly black hair piled high à la Shirley Temple began to scream. A torrent of Spanish erupted from a trio of sweating Diego Rivera–size women, two in floral muumuus, one squeezed into turquoise hot pants and a T-shirt that said "Givenchy." There was the sound of a slap. Slightly off to the side, a reed-thin thirtyish man who looked like a construction worker, with paint-spattered corduroys and skin suntanned almost to black, chain-smoked with dark haunted eyes. Presumably the father of the screamer.

After a moment, Bronwyn turned to Paul and said, with an attempt at lightness, but fearing the tone went just a bit too flat, "The marriage bureau—is this where all the world's failures come?"

"Well . . . *we're* here!" he exclaimed, taking her hand in his, rubbing it hard.

But Bronwyn became more horribly convinced of this as she

looked around and studied the crowd, began to make out the clusters and relationships. No one was young anymore, or beautiful, or in love, holding each other's hands reverently as though cradling the world's most precious gift, tilting forward toward the marriage license window like gently opening flowers. No. Everyone here seemed tired, sour-stomached, bodies literally bloated with disappointment, faces a festival of crow's-feet. It was not love that had brought them all here today but some misfortune, some awkward miscalculation, some mistake. In this sense, the marriage license was the last refuge of the beleaguered, the last gas for a hundred miles, the last bow on the coffin of one's youthful hopes.

As Paul and Bronwyn moved forward along the line—slowly, heavily, as though churning through a ride at Disneyland on a protesting rowboat, the faint odor of swamp water around them—they seemed to be drifting deeper and deeper into the World of Latino Hair. In this courtyard of zombies, as the people became sadder and more tired, the hair, by contrast, became ever more riotous, imaginative, unchained. It was the most alive thing among them. So wild became the teasing, the piling, and the dyeing that when the woman behind the window implacably handed them their license, Paul turned to Bronwyn and whispered, "Is it just me, or does she remind you of the Bride of Frankenstein?"

Bronwyn did not know if it was because this was funny, or because her stomach muscles were clenched so tightly, but all at once she felt giggles welling up inside her. Hysterical giggles.

She bit her lip, eyes tearing up, during the short, quick marriage pronouncement by the justice of the peace.

She stifled snorts of laughter when she was handed a plastic bag containing the pathetic few items the County of Los Angeles had deemed that every bride should have.

As she and Paul stumbled back out into the sun, she plunged her hand into the bag. And drew out a flyer on birth control—one side English, one side Spanish—a couple of toothbrushes, and a tiny box of Tide.

That absolutely did it.

"A tiny box of Tide," she whispered, weak. "A tiny box of Tide."

Bronwyn collapsed to her knees, tears of hilarity streaming down her face.

"For a little tiny shirt," Paul whispered, putting his long fingers side by side as if framing something.

It was just the most absurd thing.

"A tiny little shirt," she repeated, imagining it, and fell against him, snarfling with laughter.

He wrapped his arms around her, and began laughing too. Not so much because he thought it was funny, but because he was infected by the violence of her laughter. Soon his body was shaking with hers, as she laughed and wept over the ridiculousness of it.

She bent over, wheezing, and some snot pearled out of her nose. "Oh my God," she said, "I'm gross! I'm gross!"

His eyebrows went up in surprise, and now Paul was really laughing, howling . . .

And Bronwyn suddenly heard it—his trademark endearingly squeaky cadence . . .

That was it.

The thing she had missed for far too long . . . and actually forgotten.

Paul's laughter. That was the thing that had first drawn her to him. Not his face, not his wit, and certainly not his writing . . .

She had heard the laugh before even laying eyes on him at that party, before even being introduced. While not particularly loud, the cadence of Paul's laugh cut through the blaring ZZ Top music—made her stand stock-still behind a bookcase, Coors beer in hand, body frozen. "Who is *that*?" she had asked Ginny in amazement. Bronwyn couldn't even make out what direction the laughter was coming from, but it vibrated some deep chord within her, making her want to giggle and twirl in spite of herself.

Paul's laughter. That was the thing she had fallen in love with: that pure expression of fun, of joy, the thing that floated unhampered by any of the cares of the world—

And actually—she now remembered—way, way back when, that was why Paul had originally fallen in love with that ridiculous Tujunga house, their unfolding lives, and really, Los Angeles in general. Because its surprising, unexpected absurdity made him laugh. And her too, in those very early days.

She remembered their first Halloween in Tujunga, when the doorbell had rung and instead of the usual assortment of Ninja Turtles, ghosts, and Cinderellas—and even the occasional more scary gang-looking guy who would just thrust out his hands for candy—there stood two Latino boys with their floppy hair pinned rigidly up, as though they were grandmothers. They wore straight black hats, oddly prim white button-up blouses, and little elf boots. There was a shadow of chalky white makeup on their faces.

They were trying to hold very somber expressions, but they couldn't help tittering in spite of themselves.

"But what are you?" Paul had asked, as Bronwyn proffered the candy bowl.

"We're . . . Amish!" they sang out, delighted with the exotic sound of it.

And they had all laughed together at that, and laughed and laughed and laughed.

How ridiculous, Bronwyn suddenly thought, as she squinted up into the sun, and yet how sublime everything in this godforsaken city was. The senseless juxtapositions. The beach, with its ethnic families and its *Baywatch* film crew. Tudor houses next to Spanish houses next to modern cubes. The bankrupt businessmen shrilling: "Teddy bears! Teddy bears! Teddy bears!"

And how ridiculous everything in their lives in Los Angeles. Jonathan and his flea shampoo. Zibby Tanaka. Even the haplessly named Geo Futura. The Bride of Frankenstein . . .

She did not think their current financial plight was funny, of course, not at all . . .

And she knew she would not think so in one year, in five years, or maybe even in ten . . .

But at that moment, standing in the sun with her arms around her husband, Bronwyn Peters knew that eventually . . . eventually she and Paul would be sitting on chairs in front of a mobile home and they would remember it all, the whole strange episode, and they would laugh together like wrinkled old birds.

Because, as the South Dakotans said every thirty years, when yet another family fortune was lost: "After even the coldest winter has to come the spring."

And she realized that Paul's talent was not the thing that was bigger than them. It was the fact of their battered love. This was, in fact, their anchor, their subterranean continent, their floating buoy.

And now she began to weep, but weep with a kind of strange

joy, and kiss her husband, the thing she had always loved in the world more than anything.

It was a chaotic, ridiculous world, but it was theirs. It was not the world she had ever imagined, but finally it was the one they belonged in. A strange world of wind chimes and Mexican music and the heat, of roasted foods, of tattered palms. Los Angeles, the city of their beautiful dreams, their love, their youth.

Sandra Tsing Loh is a writer and monologist whose Off-Broadway solo shows include *Bad Sex with Bud Kemp* and *Aliens in America*, the latter of which was published by Riverhead in paperback. Her essay collection, the bestselling *Depth Takes a Holiday*, was also published by Riverhead. Loh is the winner of a 1995 Pushcart Prize for fiction and a MacDowell Fellowship, and is a regular commentator on NPR's "Morning Edition." "The Loh Life," her weekly radio series on KCRW, continues to document that ever-twisting thing called life in Los Angeles.